Calico

Slaughter

STAND-ALONE NOVEL

A Western Historical Adventure Book

by

Zachary McCrae

RUBEDIA
PUBLISHING

Disclaimer & Copyright

Table of Contents

Letter from Zachary McCrae

I'm a man who loves plain things: a cup of strong coffee in the morning, a good book at noon, and my wife's embrace at night.

I want to write stories that take you by the hand and show you what it meant to be someone who tried to make ends meet and find their own way in the 19th-century United States. I've been this someone for a long time in my life, always looking for my next gig after my parents' sudden death, always finding new friends, but somehow not being able to stick with 'em. It's easy to find quantity in your life, but what about quality?

At the age of 50, and after my baby boy, Jeb, and my sweet daughter, Janette, went away to study East, with my sweet wife, Mrs. Maryanne McCrae, we moved back to my hometown and my dad's ranch close to the Rockies. After a series of health issues that have brought me even closer to our Lord, I've officially started writing those stories I always loved to read.

I'm tending my land and animals now with the help of Maryanne, and I'm grateful for each day I get to walk in this world we call Earth. As the saying goes, "Nature gave us all something to fall back on, and sooner or later we all land flat on it," so I want to take care of it just the way it has taken care of my dad and mom, and my cousins.

My adventure stories are my legacy to my children and to all of the readers who will honor me by following my work. God bless you and your families and our land! Thank you.

Stay safe but adventurous,

Zachary McCrae

Prologue

Cassidy Ranch, 1853

The smoke didn't start small. It started big. High plumes of gray turned dark and ugly in the moments it took seventeen-year-old Trace Cassidy to scramble back to his horse, his heart in his mouth.

Smoke like that had to be a wildfire, didn't it? Pa had told him that they come in quick when the wind shifts. Trace jumped onto Bella, his fifteen-hand chestnut brown Saddlebred, chosen to be his first horse for her easy temper; she wasn't generally prone to skittishness.

But there was no wind today, was there? A small, errant voice inside the blond Trace's head pointed out. A moment later, Bella reared, kicking the air and throwing her head as the smell of burning reached her.

"C'mon, girl—go! You gotta go!" Trace shouted, kneeing the usually tame beast into a fitful spring, before she began galloping over the rich Colorado grasses.

No wind. And it rained last night. Bella's hooves even kicked up wet clods of soil and grass as they raced out of Little Creek, the thin ribbon of water that wound like a dropped thread across the Cassidy ranch.

No... Oh, no. Trace didn't want to think about what the smoke meant. If it wasn't a wildfire, then what was it? Had Pa dropped a lantern in the big barn? No. Trace knew his father to be a strong, mostly silent man who was capable of routing rustlers and Indians and quelling a room of disgruntled Denver men with just a look. Pa would never be so careless—but Frankie or Wade, his younger siblings, might.

What have you done, Wade? Trace snarled into the wind, immediately guessing who the culprit was.

But no sooner had Trace broken from under the cover of the elms and aspens that clustered around Little Creek, than he saw the full extent of the chaos.

It wasn't just the big barn that was on fire. And this was no wildfire.

Flames consumed the Cassidy ranch house. Red tongues flared out of every window, and the front door was a billow of black smoke. Trace couldn't even see the roof. The big barn where they stored their hay and feed was a pyre. Even the little barn and the calving shed had flames shooting up their sides.

"What—Pa! Ma!" Trace shouted—just as he heard the first shot.

Trace Cassidy had heard the sound of bullets before. He had shot enough jackrabbits himself and used a Springfield .22 rifle to scare off the coyotes that slunk around the ranch, eager to catch a newborn calf.

Somehow, these shots were different. They were sharper, louder, *angrier.*

"Mary! Get the children—"

Billows of black, choking smoke obscured Trace's vision, but it brought with it his father's strong voice, cut short by the sound of angry yells.

Pa is in there somewhere.

Pa was in danger, and Trace knew at once who was responsible.

The Rattler. The outlaw who was terrorizing western Colorado territory. Pa had tried not to talk too much about it in front of him...but Trace had overheard the name all the same. Trace had heard Pa having talks with Ezekiel Flint, at one of the next ranches over, about this 'dangerous outlaw who won't stop!'

Trace kicked Bella to gallop faster—but the smoke and the embers and the screams of cattle stuck in the barns were too much for her. Bella reared up, spittle frothing at her mouth, her eyes rolling, and Trace felt his feet slip the stirrups.

"Whoa—!"

Trace Cassidy felt a moment of weightlessness as he was thrown from the saddle—the moment stretching long in that way that total panic always causes. It was like the time Wade had fallen from the banisters he had been resolutely climbing, or when Trace had disturbed a rattlesnake and it had coiled up right before his eyes.

But just as quickly, Trace was hitting the ground with a heavy thump, and pain shook through his body, making his teeth knock together, and all breath escaped his young body.

Pa. Pa will know what to do.

Black smoke was billowing all around him now, so thick that it was impossible to see where Bella had galloped to, or even the ranch yard right in front of him. There were more sneering shouts coming from the murk—voices that Trace had never heard before.

"Pa!" Trace yelled, pushing himself up before he stupidly took a lungful of the foul air. Soot and dust filled his throat, and he hacked, doubling back over to the ground.

9

"*Pa?*" Trace gasped, his eyes streaming now. He could even feel the heat of the flames against his skin, hotter than any midsummer midday.

He had to find him. He had to find Ma, and Frankie and Wade, too. Trace pushed himself into a low run, keeping as low as possible as the smoke washed him with its char and fumes.

Trace ran to where he had last heard his father's voice, which he thought was at the end of the ranch house. He turned the corner, seeing a tunnel of smoke between the ranch house and the big barn suddenly swirling and—

"*Heeyah!*"

A horse and its rider burst through the smoke, almost striking him as Trace dove out of the way.

What?

It was no rider that Trace had ever seen before, and he didn't recognize the coal-black horse either. The man had a Stetson and a kerchief tied over his face. Trace saw flashing hooves and hurled himself to one side—but what stuck in his mind were the bright red riding gloves that the bandit wore, clutching at his reins. In the next instant, the bandit had charged past the skidding Trace and back into the smoke.

And in the man's wake, there was a huddled form on the floor.

"No. What—what is going on?" Even though he was lying down, Trace knew that form. He knew the cream work shirt that his father wore, and the brighter green neckerchief that was still around his throat.

His father lay in the dirt, and he was stone-cold dead.

Words left Trace. He didn't scream. He didn't know *how* to scream just then. His world had collapsed at the sight of his father's body, and the sound of the flames around him. For the second time that day, his world slowed almost to a standstill.

Pa was dead. He had been shot.

It was true. They were under attack.

A burst of flames and the sudden explosion of one of the upstairs windows snapped Trace out of his trance. Ma and Frankie and Wade were still out there somewhere in the smoke. He had to get to them. It was up to him to protect them now, wasn't it?

Trace knew about bandits and outlaws. Pa didn't like to talk about them in front of Trace and Wade, but one of their occasional cattle-handlers, Mr. Joseph, did. Joseph would tell Trace lurid tales of gunfights out on the Chesholm Trail, or over in the new California territories—entire towns being terrorized by bandits just as famous as the lawmen who hunted them down.

But this wasn't one of Mr. Joseph's stories, and Trace realized that Mr. Joseph himself was probably lying dead somewhere on the ranch.

Time snapped back into fast motion as Trace realized he was holding something. Looking down, through streaming eyes, he saw he had his father's Colt. He didn't even remember picking it up from the floor, but he knew it was his Pa's because it had the tooled red leather around the grip.

A gunshot broke through the ever-hungry growl of the fire, and Trace spun around. Before he had taken two steps, the shot was followed by a girl's high-pitched scream.

"Frankie!" Trace knew his sister's voice, even when it was twisted with terror.

He ran through the smoke, his father's revolver feeling oddly heavy in his hand. His shoes hit something, and he almost tripped before he jumped out of the way to skid in the dirt...to see the second worst thing he had ever seen in his life.

His mother lay dead in the dirt, a rifle half-clutched to her side, and her eyes thankfully closed.

Trace felt a low kick of horror in his stomach. His parents were dead. They were gone. There was only him, his sister Frankie, and Wade now.

And he was all that stood between the outlaws and his brother and sister.

"*No!*"

It wasn't Trace who screamed—it was Frankie's voice.

Trace spun back around to see a figure striding through the smoke, dragging his sister, Frankie, by the hair as she kicked and bawled.

Frankie had the same golden-brown hair that Trace did, with the same ragged waves in it that she was always trying to comb out.

"Lemme go!" she screamed, and tried to dig her heels into the dirt, but the man just twisted his hands in her hair.

It was the same man he had seen on the horse. Trace saw the same red leather gloves he had seen on the rider's reins.

This man had killed his parents. And now he was kidnapping his sister. It was *him*, wasn't it? It was the Rattler himself.

"*STOP! Leave her alone!*" Trace yelled. He forgot his burning lungs and the pain in his eyes. Anger coursed through him as

12

wild as any unbroken stallion. In a flash, he had brought up his father's gun.

But the bandit either hadn't heard him over the roar of the fire or didn't care. He kept on walking, and any moment, he was going to disappear into the smoke.

No.

Trace's arms trembled, but he knew he couldn't let his sister be taken from him. He couldn't let this evil man get away with what he had done.

He pulled the trigger. The recoil of the pistol was stronger than he had expected. Either that or he hadn't held the gun properly, as his hands were thrown back and he staggered to one side.

"Agh!"

Trace was rewarded with a snarl of pain as the bandit with the red gloves stumbled to one side, letting go of Frankie at once.

I hit him. Trace thought, amazed.

But the bandit had spun around, as fast as a bucking colt, and Trace saw the gleam of steel in the man's hand. He had a pistol of his own, and before Trace could even lift his aching wrist, there was a loud boom and the dirt right in front of his feet exploded.

Trace let out a yell despite himself; his legs shook as he jumped back.

I'm going to die. This man is going to kill me.

"What we got here, some little grunt wanting to play *hero*, huh?" the bandit sneered. His voice was rich and deep, but Trace couldn't see his face past the red kerchief. All he could

13

see was how broad he was, and how he was pointing that pistol right at his chest.

"You...you let go of my sister," Trace said, but even he could hear the tremor in his own voice.

The bandit cocked his head to one side, regarding Trace for one long moment as the Cassidy ranch burned behind him. Moving with glacial slowness, the man shrugged and nodded to where Frankie was on the floor a few meters away, her face pale and full of fear.

He could shoot her just as quick as he shot at me. Trace realized how stupid he had been for not killing him.

"You caught me a winger there, young pup," the man said once again in that deep, gravelly voice of his. Trace couldn't work out if that was a threat or a statement. The bandit's free hand reached up to dab at his own shoulder, but the man didn't even flinch when he touched the graze.

"You killed my parents," Trace whispered. Somehow, even amid the chaos of screaming traffic and the shouts of more loud and angry men around them—clearly this man's gang— the bandit heard him.

"I did," the bandit said evenly. He took a step forward, his gun still leveled at Trace.

*If his hand moves, I'll shoot him. I'll be as fast as those lawmen in the stories...*Trace desperately wished.

But then the bandit spoke. "You're lucky you're so small. Maybe you've got some years to grow big yet, and then maybe you'll come looking for me. *Then* we can have a proper chat about today, pup." The bandit leered at him. "But right now..? You ain't worth my time. You hear me, son? You ain't *worth* my bullets.*"

There was a chorus of harsh laughter from the smoke. More figures had stepped forward, flanking Trace. There must have been three, no four, no five more of them. They all had rifles or pistols pointing right at Trace and Frankie.

Had they been covering him the whole time? Could this man have had him killed any moment he wanted? Trace felt a little faint with shock and rage.

"You come find me when you think you're man enough, pup!" the bandit repeated with a laugh that was echoed by his gang. "But you watch your back, y'hear? Because I'm going to be keeping an eye on you. Maybe I'll come for you and your sister first, eh?"

The cruel laughter that swirled around Trace made his cheeks burn with shame. He couldn't raise his father's gun to shoot now that he was surrounded. This bandit could have done anything he wanted, and that made Trace's soul burst with guilt.

But Trace clung to one thing. The bandit hadn't said anything about his younger brother. He hadn't threatened Wade, either.

Does that mean that the bandit doesn't know that Wade exists?

"*H-yagh!*" The red-gloved bandit yelled suddenly, enough to make Trace jump as the bandits whooped and fired their guns into the air—and then they were gone, turning and running into the smoke as the black clouds billowed and bloomed all around them.

"Frankie!" All of Trace's limbs began to shake at once as he ran over to his sister, grabbing her in his arms, holding her, turning her away from the body of their mother.

"It was so quick, Trace. I didn't know anything—I smelled the burning and then it was just so quick, Trace." Frankie sobbed into his arms as Trace pulled her away from the front of the house. He could hear more gunshots and shouts and the sound of hooves stamping on the ground as the bandits left.

"Ma—" Frankie started to whisper.

"Don't. Don't think about that. Not now." Trace said at once. Somehow, it was easier to concentrate on his sister's shock than on his own. So long as he kept her safe, then maybe something good could come of this...

We have to survive. Me, Frankie, and Wade.

"Frankie, listen to me. Where's Wade? Where did you last see Wade?" Trace asked, trying to sound as certain and sure as Pa always did.

"Wade..." Frankie blinked her bright eyes, as if suddenly remembering something. "I heard Ma tell him to get to the storm shelter. But I don't know if Wade got there."

"Good enough. Let's go," Trace said, putting his arm around his sister and clamping her to him as he almost picked her up. The storm shelter was pretty much a pit out beyond the little barn that Pa had lined with wood and put a low wooden roof over, turning it into an outdoor cellar of sorts.

They stumbled out of the smoke, with Trace not slowing or stopping until he had made it past the little barn to where the storm shelter sat on the edge of the lower paddock. The smoke was still around, but the air was a little sweeter out here, and more importantly, there was no sign of the gang.

"Wade? *Wade!*" Trace called, leaving Frankie to collapse by the side of the shelter and seized one side of it, lifting it with a creak of hinges.

16

There was a movement from below him in the dark.

"Trace?"

Huddled by the ladder, Trace could see his younger brother's wide blue eyes, looking just as terrified as his sister's had. He also had the same wavy blond hair, plastered to his forehead with fear sweat.

Thank heavens. Trace breathed hard. Wade was alive. So was Frankie. They were reliant on *him* now. There was no one else to save them. He had to find a way to keep them alive through the rest of the night.

Chapter One

Chancellorsville, Virginia, 1863

"General Lee is a blowhard—" Wade said the words too loudly in the cramped carriage. Trace immediately shot him a look.

What are you spotting to do, Wade—get yourself boots up on the ground?

The Confederate carriage they were in jolted on the rutted Virginia track. The branches of overhanging birch and beech trees scraped the top of their carriage, and Trace cast a quick eye around his fellow sons of the south.

They were supposed to be in a red state, but all of Virginia had become a battleground this spring. It was easy to see why tempers were high—and why his younger brother might have misspoken. But the men around them were solemn, hard-eyed. It was hard for Trace to tell if they were huffy with Wade's nervous titter or just the fact that they were deep behind enemy lines.

Find the enemy. Monitor their positions. Report back. Trace gritted his teeth silently. Being a scout wasn't an easy job at the best of times...

"I mean, I had ears on General Hoover say as much himself. He thinks Lee's campaign is crazy," Wade went on.

Two of his fellow scouts shuffled uneasily in their seats, leaning forward with the air of men who were fit to teach through a fist to the jaw.

"Wade!" Trace hissed quickly. At once, his younger brother blinked and shut up. Wade could be a blowhard himself at the best of times, but he knew when his older brother was mad.

One of the men opposite them cleared his throat, and the tall, good-looking form of Cole Sutton leaned forward. He had black hair and the same green eyes as his sister, Annabelle, and he was one of the fellow Calico Pass Coloradans who had signed up for the war along with Trace and Wade.

He looks the spit of his sister, Trace thought. Well, with a squarer jaw and stubble that was.

"Don't you pay no mind to our whippersnapper, gentlemen. Wade always had an addle-head!" Cole laughed a little too loudly. Trace felt Wade stiffen in outrage beside him, and so he nudged him hard with his knee. Some of the scouts in this carriage were native Virginians, not out-of-state hayseeds like Trace, Wade, and Cole. Trace figured they had mighty high opinions of the brash, daring, lightning campaign of General Lee.

"Well, maybe you mind him, or I will!" one of the scouts said; a dark-haired, bushy-bearded Blue Ridge mountains guy who looked as though he could split logs with one hand.

Too far.

Trace cleared his throat and sat up a little straighter in the jostling carriage. Once again, the entire transport went quiet as he fixed Mr. Blue Ridge Lumberjack with an eye.

"Trace, don't—it's alright..." Wade whispered at once. Even Cole, opposite him, looked wary.

As well, they all might. Trace glared at the man, keeping his chin up, and made sure Mr. Blue Ridge knew that he wasn't afraid of anyone or anybody.

A second later, Mr. Blue Ridge looked away.

That's right, Trace thought. He knew he had a reputation among the soldiers, and the recent events at Chancellorsville had only cemented it.

Fourteen enemy kills. Both with rifle shot and close-at-hand, when they had to overrun their position. Trace wondered for a moment where he got it from. How he got to be so good at this.

The fire. The bandit with the red gloves. The image of burning flames swelled in his mind, and he thought he heard an echo of Frankie's screams. Even to this day, he could smell that black smoke in his nostrils when his mind wandered.

He guessed when you had everything taken away from you, there wasn't much left, was there? Trace eased back in his seat, his point proven. He nodded at Wade and Cole.

Nothing left apart from these people, of course. Trace had been angry when Wade had followed him into the Confederacy. But his little brother was a wild card, and he was also a young man now. Trace knew there was nothing he could do to stop him once he got his mind set on something.

Apparently, that something was the endless civil war ripping their United States of America apart.

Trace was lost in these thoughts when the carriage suddenly jolted, throwing everyone a little.

"What is that?" Wade hissed quickly, rubbing a hand through his wavy blond hair—the same gesture Trace knew he did himself when he was worried.

"We're not meant to stop until Bealeton." Trace's hand reached for the door to the carriage.

Stopping on the road was bad. They were trying to head north quickly, to then embark on foot towards the last known enemy position. Rumor was they were heading for Gettysburg, but it would take weeks to move their forces that far.

Something must have gone wrong. Trace flickered a glance at the other eight scouts.

"Stay here," he added tersely. He nodded to Cole to come with him. Trace had known Cole since they were chillun, and Trace would rather have a man he knew the grit of beside him.

"Brother—" Wade, of course, started to argue, but Trace silenced him with a look.

Not you. You think I'm not spending every hour of my day trying to keep you alive? He didn't say it, but he didn't have to as Wade sat back, glowering.

Trace was the first out of the carriage, his rifle primed and ready as his boots hit the trail dirt. There were deep ruts in this track through the woods. It was clear it was used for carts, but wasn't wide enough for two of them.

He turned to the drivers, and that was when Wade burst out of the carriage behind him, hurriedly checking his rifle.

"Little brother, I told you to hold back!" Trace hissed, but a sight ahead of the stalled and uneasy carriage was more important right now.

His brother offered him one of his famous reckless grins. "You take your chances in this life, Trace. Didn't you teach me that?"

Trace shot him an annoyed look. Yes, he *had* told him that. But it didn't mean that you had to run into danger!

There was a tree down across the road. Its white bark was scattered with black nodules. Most of its branches were still intact, but its base had been hacked with fresh ax chops.

Oh no.

Trace was already turning back when he caught sight of their singular driver sitting up front *with a damn arrow sticking out of his neck!*

"Attack!" Trace managed to holler, just as the first volley of bullets screamed out of the trees.

Trace dove backwards towards his brother, but he was too slow. He saw the bullet take him on the shoulder, throwing him against the carriage with a strangled yell.

"Wade!" Trace shouted. He skidded to his brother's side, twisting to fire a round into the woods, as figures jumped out towards him.

Hells!

It was mayhem. Trace dropped to his knee beside his brother's groaning form, discarding the rifle to grab his Colt revolver instead, and firing two shots at the racing men as Cole took out one with his first rifle shot.

By now, the rest of Trace's scouts were jumping from the carriage, and they had wisely chosen their revolvers for such close combat instead of their rifles. Still, the Union forces had the element of surprise. Mr. Blue Ridge Mountains went down in the first hail of bullets, and Paulo, a young man who had somehow come up all the way from the Mexican border, fell second.

"Hold on, Wade!" Trace snarled. In an instant, he knew they had to break the ambush. And the only way to do that was...

"*Yeller-bellied varmints!*" Trace howled as he grabbed his rifle in his free hand, diving forward into the mass of oncoming men. One bullet went into a Union belly, and his rifle stock cracked another in the knee, bringing him down.

Trace was surrounded by the Union soldiers. Visions of flame poured through his eyes. He heard the echo of mocking laughter.

'*When you're man enough, young pup—*'

He gave himself up to his fury. Pa had always said he had a temper on him.

And by God, today am I proving it!

Trace whirled, slamming the rifle butt into the fork of another man's legs before dropping it, firing once again straight up at another. He was surrounded by angry, shocked, leering faces of men he would never know, but he would send to hell for daring to attack his little brother.

"Charge!" He recognized the shout of one of his fellow scouts as he realized he was now on top of one of the Unionists, slamming his head against the dirt before stealing the man's gun. What happened to his own? Didn't matter. All that mattered was Wade.

The Confederate scouts had rallied, hitting the Union ambush with their bayonets and pistols and knives. Trace's unhinged attack had cut a hole through their middle, and a moment later, what was left of the enemy was turning tail and running for the tree line.

"Wade!" Trace pushed the body of the Union soldier off him, lunging to his feet to race back to the carriage. Wade was only a few meters away, lying on the dirt by the side of the open carriage door like a sack of dropped potatoes.

No—

"Trace, *lookit!*" one of his buddies shouted, but it wasn't fast enough.

Something hit Trace's head with all the force of a cannonball. With his eyes still on Wade, Trace fell forward, and into darkness.

Chapter Two

Chancellorsville, Virginia, 1863

Wade.

WADE!

Trace smelled black smoke and heard his sister screaming as he snarled, grabbing the attacker that got in his way.

"Specialist. *Specialist!* Get a hold of yourself, it's Officer Cooper!"

Trace's vision cleared, and he saw that the man holding him down wasn't some faceless Union soldier (and it wasn't the red-gloved bandit, either); it was none other than Captain Cooper, his direct superior.

Jakob Cooper was an older man with a full gray mustache, but short, balding gray hair receding in the middle. He was hard and had a soul of steel, and Trace liked that.

"My brother," Trace gasped, as the next thing he was aware of was a monumental headache blossoming across his temples.

Oh yeah. He had been shot, hadn't he? It felt like his head was about fit to fall off, and now that he remembered it, he felt the thick rolls of bandage wrapped against his head.

"You were real lucky, son. Bullet damn near grazed you. Either you got an angel or someone's looking after you up there." Cooper gestured vaguely towards the ceiling of the tent, where apparently all good and noble things dwelt.

Trace didn't have time to think about angels. "My brother," he repeated, sitting up and reaching for the edge of the bed. He was in a Confederate medical tent, and he guessed probably back around Chancellorsville, as the army had yet to move off from the successful battle site they had just taken.

As soon as he moved, a wave of vertigo hit him, and he clenched his teeth in a hiss of pain and anger.

"Easy there, Specialist. You ain't going nowhere. Not until the doc gives you the a-okay," Cooper repeated, turning around to cast a glance around the rest of the room. Trace realized he was in a private, sheeted-off area of a medical tent. *Why?*

"Now listen up, Cassidy. You're a damn fine soldier, and that is why I came down here myself to inform you." Cooper turned abruptly back towards him. Wade felt a sinking feeling in his chest.

No-no-no.

"Corporal Cole Sutton, who I know signed up for you, perished due to his wounds on the Bealeton Road." Cooper said.

Not Cole! Trace remembered his easy-going nature and the way he matched Wade's more volatile friendship so easily. The Suttons and the Cassidys had been as thick as thieves, once.

"And your brother, too—" Jakob Cooper kept on speaking, but the words disappeared into a roar of white noise. Trace's vision threatened to go dark around the edges as the bitter pain hit him.

His brother was dead. Wade Cassidy had succumbed to his wounds on the road to Bealeton. But he would be given a military burial, and the next three months of Wade's pay would be credited to Trace...

This couldn't be happening. Not again.

A haze of red threatened to take over. Trace's mind swirled with remembered flames and the screams of those he loved. This world had taken Pa and Ma, and now it had taken Wade too...

"I'm going to kill them!" Trace snarled. He found he was standing up, and the pain in his head was just a distant echo. He knew that nothing was going to stop him. He would find the Union unit that did this to his family, and he would-

"Not so fast, Specialist." Cooper's gravel-filled voice cut through Trace's rage. "I'm not having you gallivanting out there on some half-assed revenge mission. That unit that came for you was one of the Union's best. Experienced scouts. You'll get yourself killed."

"No, I won't." Trace glared at the captain.

Cooper's eyes narrowed. "I'll forget you looked at me like that, soldier, on account of the recent news and all."

But Trace couldn't back down. He ignored his returning headache. All that he felt was rage.

"You just said this unit is dangerous. A substantial threat, and they are right in our territory. Let me take the men and hunt them down. Two birds—one stone." Trace said.

They took my brother. Surely the man in you understands what I have to do? Trace thought.

The captain looked at him for a moment longer, his eyes shadowed. Trace was sure Cooper was going to deny him.

"We'll talk in the morning, Specialist." Cooper snapped and turned to march out of the medical room.

***

27

"Dead ahead?" Trace whispered to his fellow Confederate scout, kneeling in the forest mulch beside him. Fingers of morning fog were still penetrating through the trees. It was early, so early that dawn was nothing but a gray smear through the eastern trees.

They had found them. The Union unit who called themselves 'the *Sharps*' – probably a reference to their repeating, breech-loaded rifles.

Useless for long-distance shots, Trace thought scornfully.

His fellow scout nursed his own long rifle, lying in a scrape against the side of a tree, pointing down at the haze of mist and campfires below them.

"We can't see spit," his man muttered. Trace didn't mind the criticism. Soldiers had a way of talking freely with each other like that.

"They'll come running. All you have to do is keep on firing." Trace told the man exactly what he had just told the other scout a few meters to his left, and so on, and so on.

Cooper had only given him a handful of men for the mission, and they were only supposed to find the Sharps, not engage.

But Trace had briefed his men himself. They were going to strike a blow against the Union, and in particular, these men who had killed his brother and probably his closest friend.

"Ready when you are, sir," the scout grunted, setting his revolver on the ground beside him, so it was easy to pick up if the fighting got close.

"You'll know my signal," Trace promised, stealing away from the man and creeping between the trees, moving slowly to avoid slipping on the wet mulch. If the soldier had been alarmed by his sudden movement, then the man was too well-disciplined to say anything.

Trace's heart burned with fury. He was silent in the night. A killer. He reached on hand into the pouch at his side and drew forth his secret weapon.

It looked like a dart, with a wooden tail and a large, heavy, oval head made of iron.

A grenade.

In his other pocket, he had the large packet of black powder, and Trace didn't even feel a hint of danger as he crept nearer and nearer to the glow of enemy camp fires.

It had cost him a pretty penny to get this grenade out of the Arms Store, as grenades were rare on their side. This was only one from a box of ten that the entire Arms Store had available.

Trace's face was fixed in a rictus grin of savagery as he crept closer and closer. He saw the first looming shadow of the Union tents appearing out of the mist. The Sharps had chosen a clearing to camp in for the night.

It was going to be their last.

When Trace was sure that he was close enough, he ducked down to unscrew the cap and fill the iron device with the black powder. He thought of Wade, and of Cole, as he poured it.

These men had hurt him *bad*. And now they were going to pay.

When it was filled, he carefully placed the percussion cap back in rose from his crouch.

"Gerrit?"

He heard a sleepy murmur of a voice down there in the camp. He didn't care. These animals had taken everything from him.

As the memory of flames filled Trace's mind, he uncurled like a striking cougar. His arm shot out—the grenade soared over the tents—straight into the central camp fire.

Trace dropped to the floor just as the boom hit, with a powerful flash of light and flame that set his ears ringing. He didn't pause. People were screaming, and there was the smell of smoke in his nose as he jumped forward, drawing his Colt .45 and starting on what he came here to do.

"Attack!"

"Where?"

Shouts rose around him as Trace jumped forward between the smoking and charred remains of the tents. He was a hunting wolf as he ran down the avenues between the canvas, hip-shooting every Union soldier who appeared in front of him.

At some point, his gun ran out of bullets, and it would take too long to reload. He was drunk on revenge as he jumped into the crater of the flower, hitting the dirt with a roll to snatch up one of the dropped revolvers of his enemy.

"You!"

There was an angry shout behind him. Trace spun in time to see a man emerging out of the smoke and mist. The man was bulky and tall. He had a red kerchief held to his head.

And Chicken Guts, Trace saw the golden braid on the man's jacket. The man was an officer. Not just an officer—the captain of the unit, and he had recognized Trace from the ambush. Guns roared in the night as Trace's men fired on the fleeing *Sharps*.

This man had killed Cole. He had taken Wade from him.

Trace didn't even think about it—he shot the captain of the *Sharps* dead before he hit the ground.

***

"Trace! You did it!"

"He did it—they're sowing daisies!"

Trace next came to his senses with the sounds of his own men cheering as they rushed him, grabbing him, and pulling him to his feet.

Where am I?

Oh yeah. He had been sitting on the ground before the dead captain and the utter destruction of the Union camp. He had almost single-handedly routed them, and his small gang of fellow scouts had done the rest.

So this is what victory feels like, Wade thought as he looked at the churned mud and the bodies all around him. Strange thing was, he didn't feel a thing. That awful anger in his heart had gone—but in its place was nothing but a great big hole, and he still smelled black smoke and felt the heat of flames threatening nearby.

Huh?

"Top rail, Trace—*top rail!*" The same scout he had talked to before he had attacked was saying, almost jumping up and down in delight.

Trace looked at him, and strangely, he couldn't find anything in himself to share in the man's enthusiasm. He knew distantly that this was a good thing, that they had won—but then why did he feel so lost?

"Just—just give me a moment." Trace muttered, breaking free from the men who were starting to holler and howl with excitement as they looted the dead.

"Is this what I have become?" Trace whispered, stumbling to the edge of the woods and falling down on his knees. The sky had lightened now, with the imminent arrival of the sun.

He could see the handiwork of his actions clearly.

Trace thought about the strong man that his father had been. He thought about the care that his father had put into trying to teach them all to do better, be better.

'There's a whole lot of evil out there in the world, Trace. You remember that, huh? That's why God wants each and every one of us to be upstanding. We gotta do the work down here, you see?'

His father's long-ago words floated back to him. And when Trace considered what he saw around him, he knew this was not what his father would have done.

"Dear God, help me see your divine justice. Make me a man like my father," Trace prayed.

Chapter Three

Colorado City, Colorado Territories, 1866

"All depart! Colorado City, here we are!"

The cry of the driver disturbed Trace from where he had been leaning against the wagon canvas, pretending to sleep. In truth, he just didn't want to have to spend another moment talking to his fellow soldiers. An air of defeat clutched at them, sharpened by the fact that each of them had only been given a meager pittance of what was owed them.

We lost. In truth, Trace wasn't surprised. The Union Army had been better equipped and had more money. The South, although more daring, hadn't really managed to get back on its feet after Gettysburg.

The Confederate Army was broke by the end of the war. Trace had been sent home with the end of his month's pay, and that was it. No out-payment as the Union soldiers got (or so he heard).

Either way, his fellow soldiers brightened a little now they had arrived in Colorado territory. The city had been notorious even when Trace had been growing up, and Pa had forbidden him or Wade to visit it for years.

The sounds of rye-soaked laughter and the heavier, acrid scent of opium met him as Trace stepped down from the wagon and tipped his hat to the driver. He didn't have a horse, so it would be a fair walk back to the ranch.

Home. Trace still couldn't believe it. It felt like he had been gone a lifetime, not years. How could he ever tell Frankie everything that he had seen?

Wade. Cole.

For a moment, Trace smelled that black smoke once again. Why couldn't he have saved them? Why didn't he see it coming?

He had written Frankie about it, of course. She was the first to know about their brother—and about her husband-to-be.

It had been only natural that Frankie and Cole Sutton had gotten sweet on each other, Trace thought. Their families had known each other since any of the chillun were big enough to walk on their own two feet, after all.

"Hey! That's you, ain't it?" A bleary voice shouted from one of the many saloons that decorated Colorado City's main street. Trace looked around to see a man in a striped poncho with whiskers and stubble he hadn't bothered to shave for a good while. From the way he lurched as he stood up from the saloon porch, Trace figured his belly was already full of the strong stuff.

"Do I know you, buddy?" Trace said. He didn't recognize the man, and he figured he knew most of the original ranchers and homesteaders on the outskirts of the city. No—this was a newcomer, like most of the Confederate soldiers that he had traveled here with.

"You're the Devil of Bealeton, aren't ya? I was at Chancellorsville—I saw you take the rise. And then I heard you put the Sharps underground, all by yerself!" The man's voice grew louder. It was impossible for the others in the street not to hear him.

"The devil? Is that him, really?"

"Think you got the wrong man, fella." Trace grimaced, turning hurriedly to grab his knapsack and his walking rod. The sooner he was out of this accursed place, the better.

"Trace?"

A much lighter voice cut through the hubbub of the street. Trace would recognize that voice anywhere.

"Frankie!" He spun around to see his sister walking onto the main street, leading two horses behind her. His sister was just as he remembered—but an older version. She had managed to tame her golden hair into a queue, and she wore full green skirts instead of the overalls she used to favor.

In a heartbeat, Trace took wide, lunging steps towards her and caught his sister in a fierce hug. He felt a sob run through her body.

"I know," he said. "Wade, Cole..."

"Yeah." Frankie agreed. She broke off to hold him at arm's length as she looked at him. She frowned. "You're starting to get a bit gray there, brother. Pa went gray early, too."

At the mention of their father, Trace felt his heart tighten. *It's up to me now,* he promised, just as he had that night outside the Sharp's camp. He had to be the one to look after what was left of his family. He had to do things the right way from now on.

"I knew the Union carriages had been coming in all week, so I was hoping to catch you," Frankie said by way of explanation as she led them back to the horses, who Trace saw were old Mountbatten, the seventeen-hand Bay, and a younger horse he didn't recognize.

"New horses? The ranch has been doing well, then?" Trace asked. In truth, he had been worried. Word was that soldiers had turned outlaw after the war ended and had been roaming the country, raising hell.

Like Red Gloves? A shadow passed over his mind. He brushed it aside. The Rattler was old news.

"Oh," Frankie sniffed, and looked about ready to cry once more, but Trace saw her resolve as she hardened her jaw. She was a Cassidy woman, after all. Trace guessed that she had already done a deal of her crying over Cole and Wade. There would be more to come, maybe, but Trace could see the way that sorrow had etched its lines under Frankie's eyes.

"Actually—not so good," Frankie told him as they took the side street out of Colorado City. Trace was only too pleased to put those brothels and whiskey joints behind him.

No, what he needed was...*There!*

The wind turned, bringing with it the fresh Colorado breeze. There was nothing like it. It had a lick of cold, where it came down from the Colorado Mountains, but there were the traces of wildflowers and grasslands in it, too. Trace took a deep lungful, looking up at the rising hills ahead of them, whose sides were dotted with trees.

Peace, maybe.

"Not so good?" Trace shot a glance at his sister to see her eyes set on the trail ahead, and looking beyond it.

"Rustlers came through not a week ago, Trace," Frankie said. The wind blew a little fiercer, turning a bit colder.

"Rustlers?"

Frankie turned to him, her eyes haunted. "They took half our heads of shorthorn. *Half,* Trace!" His sister clenched her jaw. He saw the shame shake her and knew that feeling well. "Someone was shot down in Colorado City just last month.

Word is that there's a gang nearby, and Trace. " Frankie's voice faltered as she pulled her Bay to a stop.

"They say it's the Rattler. They say he's back, Trace."

"What?" Trace raised an eyebrow. No. The man who had attacked their ranch? The one who had killed their parents?

The fresh Colorado breeze was replaced by the smell of smoke in Trace's mind, and screams from long ago.

"It can't be. That was more than ten years ago," Trace scoffed. "He's got to be dead by now."

Trace had searched for the man who had taken his parents. He had ridden down into Colorado City afterwards, and he had asked questions and gotten into fights and made a name for himself. Perhaps the *Devil of Bealeton* hadn't been too far off, but he had never found him. The Rattler had disappeared just as quickly as he had appeared. He terrorized western Colorado for one long, hot summer and then, just like that, the Rattler disappeared.

And that was a long time ago, so whoever this new attacker was—it couldn't be the Rattler, could it?

"What about the sheriff?" Trace gripped his reins tightly as they started trotting forward.

"Sheriff Jackson?" Frankie pulled a face. The man was mostly known for his slow nature and his love of big meals. He turned a blind eye to the many manners of iniquity and upset that went on in Colorado City for the most part. Trace remembered Pa saying that Sheriff Jackson was a weak man given too great a task.

"We'll get through it," Trace said, as he glared hard at the horizon. "I'm back now, and I'm going to keep you safe."

Frankie's talk turned to smaller matters on their last miles up to the ranch. She told him how old man Sawyer—their pa's best friend—had lost his wife Elsie to an illness last year, and so he and his son Harlan were spending more time on the Cassidy ranch now, helping out with everything from the cattle to the buildings.

And then, Trace started to recognize the landscape around them. There was the old sycamore that he used to climb all summer long. Running along the ridge were the top meadows. And nestled below those was..

Little Creek, Trace recognized. And that meant that just a little way past the bend was...

His family ranch was nestled under the old elm tree just as it had been since forever. The elm was twisted and crooked, and one side of it had never truly grown back since the fire. But Sawyer and his son, Harlan Dagger, had done a wonderful job of putting their ranch building back together afterward. Two stories of wooden panels stood in front of him, with perfect square windows, and there was the faintest trace of white smoke pluming from the central chimney.

"Frankie? Is that...?"

His front door banged, and a striking woman walked out onto his porch. Trace blinked in surprise.

Annabelle Flint had grown up into a truly remarkable woman, by all accounts. Long black hair hung wild past her shoulders, and she had grown into her curves now. Trace remembered her as a grubby, skinned-kneed kind of girl who had always glared at him when their parents had got together.

The Flints owned one of the ranches on the other side of the Calico Pass, edging onto the deep woods.

"Oh, Trace—I should have said..." Frankie murmured.

Said what? Trace wondered.

"Trace Cassidy. I see you saw fit to head back home again after that stupid war." Annabelle said tartly. She raised her chin at him, as if she was throwing him a personal challenge.

Huh? Why was Annabelle Flint, of all people, mad at him for going to war! Trace instantly felt a flare of anger. What did she know of war? What did she know of losing people?

"Annabelle," Trace said evenly.

"Your sister's been in danger while you were away playing soldier, Trace!" Annabelle said vehemently.

Trace felt like he had been slapped. He didn't want to admit how much that hurt, and that made him even more angry, in truth.

"No one was playing, Annabelle," Trace growled. He trotted his horse to a stop and turned to hiss at Frankie, loud enough so that Annabelle could hear too. "What is *she* doing here? Hasn't she got her own home to go to?"

His sister's mouth fell open. She looked at him like he had just about said the worst thing he could ever say about anyone. "Oh, Trace..." Frankie whispered, horrified.

"What?" This was like being a teenager again.

There was a thump as Annabelle turned and slammed their door as she went back into their house.

"What's gotten into her bonnet?" Trace said.

"You don't understand..." Frankie hissed quickly, but before she could finish, his own front door slammed once again as Annabelle returned, this time hauling a large knapsack over one shoulder and a satchel on the other. She had clearly been staying here, Trace realized.

"Someone's attacking all the ranches around here, Trace Cassidy. And most of the menfolk went off to fight in that darn war. People are dying back here, Cassidy—and it's the Rattler. He's back." Annabelle threw the words at him.

Visions of flames filled Trace's mind. He remembered angry, leering shouts as shapes emerged from the smoke. *No.*

"Those are just scare stories." Trace shut down that suggestion. He couldn't have the Rattler in his life. He *wouldn't.*

"The Rattler is long gone. Probably buried in a dirt grave somewhere, hopefully. You're just being paranoid, Anna," Trace said firmly.

Annabelle flinched as if slapped, and her cheeks turned a bright red. Then, without saying a word, she turned and stalked across the porch, hopping the end as she marched to the Cassidy stables. A few moments later, there was an angry cry, and she emerged on her dappled blue mare, breaking into a fast trot as soon as she was in the yard, which turned into a gallop when she had passed Trace and Frankie.

"What's her problem?" Trace grumbled.

Chapter Four

Calico Pass, Colorado Territory, 1866

Trace. Cassidy.

Annabelle's thoughts were a blur of anger and outrage as she leaned into the wind, and her speckled Appaloosa, Constance, threw her head a little. They galloped over the open plains, the wind whipping Annabelle's black hair behind her, and the sagebrush and yellow ox-eye flowers whipping past in a blur.

"He came back more of a fool than when he left!" Annabelle announced to no one but her horse, and in return, Constance snorted.

"Ach. Okay, okay." Annabelle eased off on her hard riding, slowing Constance into a canter, and then to a trot. The lowest hills that led up to the Calico Pass itself rose on her left, speckled with the purple sage or ochre bluff and green that gave the place its name.

But Trace. Josiah. Cassidy! Annabelle still fumed. She used his middle name like it was an accusation, because she thought she had known the man right from his very beginnings.

Their trot took them to the patch of beech woods under the hills that Annabelle had always adored. Trust Constance to know where to go when she didn't, she thought.

"You reminding me to calm down, girl?" Annabelle said wryly, slowing to a walk as they reached the eaves of the woods, before dismounting with a heavy sigh. Connie whickered slightly and reached up to steal a few of the youngest beech leaves from the lowest branches.

Annabelle patted her side distractedly. She still fumed.

"He doesn't even know what happened because he didn't bother to ask!" Annabelle grumbled to herself as she took out her water pouch and decided to leave Constance on a long rein out here.

"No, 'Hello Annie! How are you? Gosh, I've missed you these last five or six odd years—how have you been?'" Annabelle explained to Connie, who wisely chose to say nothing.

In truth, a part of Annabelle knew that there was probably nothing that anyone *could* say. What was she supposed to tell them when they asked her?

'Oh, fine, thanks, apart from the Rattler killing my entire family and almost torching my entire ranch!'

Shame, anger, and fear clutched at her heart so hard that Annabelle hissed. Her stomach ached with the bitter feelings of it, but it still made her body shake.

It had been almost a year ago now, back when the war had been raging so fierce and hard that everyone thought it would never end, and that there wouldn't even be a country left for anyone to take.

Annabelle stood, looking into the middle distance, clutching the water pouch to her chest as she saw the billows of flames and heard the cruel, mocking laughter of the man called the Rattler.

The bandit had struck in the middle of the night, as he always did. Setting fire to the Sutton's main barn. Now Annabelle knew that had been to draw them out. She scowled.

Shame bloomed through her. Why hadn't she known that was what was so obviously going to happen? Her father, along with old man Cassidy, had been the most vocal across the city in confronting the Rattler. The bandit had taken out Trace, Frankie, and Wade's parents years ago...and then he had come for hers, the last strong homesteaders left to stand up against him.

The Rattler's attacks were always the same, weren't they? First, he set fire to someplace, then he came for the people and cattle. Just like before. Just like what had happened to the Cassidys. Annabelle shook her head in annoyance. Hadn't she heard that there had been a ranch fire the other month? Heading up towards Denver? And what about that man who got shot in Colorado City?

"Not again." Annabelle's heart lurched.

There wasn't a day that went by that Annabelle didn't remember that night. She remembered fleeing over the open fields afterward, her fists scraped and blood under her nails from having to fight her way out. She remembered running here, to the Cassidy ranch.

Because the Cassidys were always good to us Suttons. They were family, in a way.

Or had been.

"What a fool I've been, thinking that the man was going to be anything like the boy," Annabelle murmured, as she tied up Connie and took the small trail that she had walked a hundred times before. She always felt better in this little patch of woods. There was something about the bright golden light hitting the beech leaves that made her thoughts quieter, and eased the sound of cruel laughter in her ears...

Her steps were enfolded by the beech wood's embrace. Annabelle's feet crunched on dried leaves and beech husks, as giant roots broke and surfaced, knotted, and disappeared once more. There, a little way ahead, was a cone of light coming through the canopy. She neared the secluded meadow where her pa used to bring her.

Now you never will, will you? Annabelle thought. Another last thing. She had thought she had given up finding them by now, one year after her father's death.

"I wish you were here, Pops," she said out loud as she stepped out into the secluded, tree-bound meadow. The air hummed with insects, and brighter wildflowers seemed to float over the top of the grass.

She walked out until she was right in the center, exactly where her father used to take her, and got her to look up.

The sky was a brilliant blue, and framed by the edges of the trees like it was in a picture.

"You would know what to do, wouldn't you?" Annabelle murmured to the sky before she let herself sink down to her knees.

The Rattler was back. After all these years, the man with the red gloves had returned, and now all hell was going to break loose.

Annabelle's eyes hardened as she looked out into the darkness between the trees.

And if Trace Cassidy wasn't man enough to do something about it—then she would!

Chapter Five

Cassidy Ranch, Colorado, 1866

"You don't know." Frankie was looking at him in horror.

"What?" Trace growled back. He hadn't just dragged himself through an entire war, dodging bullets and cannon shot to be glared at by his little sis.

"She lost her family. She lost almost everything to the Rattler." Frankie moved to him, putting her hand gently on her shoulder. The tenderness his sister could display at times broke his heart. He hadn't seen a lot of tenderness over the last few years.

"What? Old Mr. Flint? Gary? Kaylee?" Trace felt like he had just been shot. Only this time, there was no pain, just the dull shock as his world turned upside down.

Frankie was shaking her head. "It happened last year, while you were away. The Rattler fired up her ranch—just like he did ours…"

"*Don't.*" Trace heard the leering voices and once again saw the shadows emerging out of the smoke. Despite everything he had been through, he could still remember perfectly the feeling of that scared little boy, trying to lift the heavy gun to protect his family.

"It can't be the Rattler. You know that as well as I do, Frankie. I searched for him. All those years, I *searched,* and he was a darn *ghost!*" Trace gripped the horse's reins a little too tight, and she neighed in alarm.

"Annabelle knows what she saw, Trace. You remember how the Flints and Pa were. They were tight, like brothers, and they both wanted an end to the Rattler," Frankie said.

Trace shook his head. He didn't want to hear it. What was all this foolishness? He pulled on his horse's reins to lead her to the stable. She stamped in agitation.

"They killed her family, but they—they kept her a while, I think." Frankie's voice broke, and once again she was sobbing.

I'll kill them! Trace felt the terrible cold of fury run through him.

"She fought free and found her way here—" Frankie was saying, when there was a loud shout from the end of the yard.

Two riders were approaching, and for a moment, Trace's hand swept to the revolver at his belt—until he saw the big grin of someone he had thought he would never see again.

"Sawyer!" Trace yelled, more than happy for a change in subject.

"Trace! You got big, I see." Sawyer Dagger was a big man with dark skin and eyes that could pierce your soul. His son, Harlan, was probably going to be the spit of him when he grew older.

"Long legs!" Harlan jumped off his horse and was the first to greet his old friend with a fierce hug.

Home. This was what it felt like, Trace thought.

"We've been keeping an eye on the ranch, just like we promised your pa," Sawyer said, casually dismounting and taking the reins of both his and Harlan's horse, almost as an afterthought. He tipped his hat to Frankie at the same time, but then frowned when he saw Frankie's reddened eyes.

"Ah. D'you two need a minute?" Sawyer said heavily, and instantly it was just like it had been ever since Pa and Ma had gone. The Daggers had stepped in to be their family just as much as the Flints had done—more so, actually, given the fact that the Daggers lived on the Cassidy land and pretty much ran the ranch after Trace and Frankie's parents had gone. Sawyer Dagger was both sensitive and strong. The sort of man that his father had always wanted Trace to turn into.

"I just told Trace about Annabelle," Frankie blurted out.

"Ah," Sawyer said again, his brow lowering. "That's a mighty big bite of news to swallow for any man."

Sawyer's eyes flickered over to Trace. He saw the sympathy in them—and for some reason, that made Trace feel even more mad.

"I know. It's all manner of awful," Trace let out at once. He felt his heart hammering in his chest. "I don't think I'll ever forgive myself for not being here when you all needed me. But it's *not* the Rattler," Trace said starkly.

It couldn't be. Not after all these years.

"Brother—" The younger Harlan looked nervously between Trace and Frankie. "It's true, Trace. The gangs are back. There've been attacks up and down the territory, with cattle being stolen, and ranches being set fire to. Anyone with a claim, particularly in gold country, has got a story to tell."

Gold country. Trace tried not to spit. That was one of the names for this part of Colorado territory, all because some lucky panhandlers managed to make their fortune once every blue moon. It was most of the reason why Colorado City was where it was, and was *like* it was, with the foolish and the desperate coming out here to wild country in order to try and strike it rich before their savings ran out.

"The Rattler was gone a long time ago," Trace insisted. "It's more likely to be deserters from the war, breaking in and stealing food and whatever else they can get their hands on."

Harlan, who had always been the first to laugh and shout and holler as a kid, now had a somber look on his face.

"Maybe so, Trace. Maybe so. Sheriff Jackson says we might be looking at a couple of gangs in the area. Some of the attacks include burnings, others are mostly people getting jumped on the trails."

Trace turned away from his friend. He didn't want Harlan to see his look of scorn, not on the first day he had seen him for over five years.

Burnings. Just like the Rattler used to do.

"Sheriff Jackson is looking into it?" Trace said quickly. He didn't know if he was filled with confidence by that. The sheriff hadn't been much good for them all those years ago when the Rattler *really had* been here.

"Uh-huh," Harlan nodded.

Trace let out a groan. A wave of exhaustion rolled through him. He rubbed his eyes.

Sawyer suddenly cleared his throat, nodding to Harlan. "Son? Help Miss Cassidy with the supplies I see over there— and Trace? Can you help an old man take these horses in?" he asked.

Trace knew what he was doing. He was clearly just trying to give him a job to take his mind off things. It was a kindness, but it was obvious.

"You're hardly old, Dagger," Trace said, but he took the reins off Frankie's Bay and his own as Sawyer walked his and Harlan's horse to the large Cassidy stable block.

It was just like old times, in a weird way. Apart from the news that half of Colorado City was under attack. Trace couldn't count the amount of times he had stabled the horses like this with Sawyer.

They walked into the familiar darkness, and the horses whickered softly at the promise of fresh hay and fodder. Trace fell into a rhythm he had thought he'd forgotten, as he led the horses to their stalls, took off their saddles, and got the brushes as Sawyer forked fresh sweet grass and hay into each feed bag. Soon, they were surrounded by the sound of chomping and gentle breathing.

"It must have been hard, out there," Sawyer admitted.

Trace winced. He had been waiting for this chat, and he had told himself he was going to resent it—but in truth, the familiarity of Sawyer's voice eased his nerves.

"Sounds like hard times back here, too." Trace said. He thought of Annabelle. He shouldn't have been so harsh on her.

"Aye, but nothing like a war. You know *my* father and *your* father's father were both in the big one, don't you?" Sawyer said.

"The War of Independence," Trace said, in almost hushed terms. It was funny hearing those words, considering what he had just seen out there. There wasn't anything holy or hallowed about war.

"That's right. The Daggers and the Cassidys go way back. The stories our fathers told would chill your blood." Sawyer shot him a hard look. "Or maybe they wouldn't. Not now."

Trace didn't say anything. What was there to say about grown men and barely grown men fighting and dying in muddy ditches, far from home?

"I miss your brother," Sawyer said.

"So do I," Trace admitted. His breath twisted in his throat.

"I miss Cole, too. It's a terrible thing, being surrounded by death—" Sawyer started to say.

No.

Trace let out a strangled cough and shook his head. He felt hot, angry, and ashamed. His brother had died, and it was his fault. His sister's fiancé had died, and he should have protected him. His pa and now Annabelle's family...

"I know what you're doing, Sawyer, and I'm not doing it," Trace said through gritted teeth. He turned around, looking for a way out of here and away from the man's deep, kind eyes. "The world is a hard place," Trace offered, clicking to his horse, who looked mournfully at her feed bag, before she lifted up her head and came to be saddled. "I'm going for a ride. Need to clear my head." Trace growled, getting the horse ready in a rush as Sawyer looked on.

Trace was leading his steed back out of the stables when Sawyer's voice found him.

"Your father was very proud of you, Trace Josiah Cassidy!" Sawyer said.

Trace flinched and kept on walking. Somehow, those words only stung more than a thousand gunshot wounds.

Was he, though?

***

Trace took the horse out onto the land, and for a while, he just rode. He didn't think. He didn't even tell the horse where to go, but blindly selected whatever trail was in front of him.

It felt good to be in the saddle again. When he was younger, he had barely gone a day without riding.

All that had changed with the war, of course, where the soldiers were expected to march or be carried on wagons.

The plains around him were a spectacular display of greens and oranges and purples. On his right, he could see the majestic rise of the Colorado mountains, tipped in white, and the tiny spur of the Calico Pass as his horse picked her path.

Finally, Trace felt like he could breathe again. All he could smell was good, clean dirt and fresh mountain air.

His horse slowed, snorting gently. Trace looked up to Annabelle's dappled Appaloosa tied on a long rope to the last tree of the old beech wood.

"Oh, darn it." Trace eased to a slow walk. His cheeks burned. He hadn't meant to follow her out here, and it seemed that she must like this old place as much as he remembered it.

But the ride had cleared some of the anger from Trace's mind. He felt shame for how he had spoken to her.

"Now that I know what she's lost," he murmured, clicking his horse forward, before he dismounted and carefully tied her up beside the speckled mare.

"I'll only tell her I'm sorry, then I'll go," he murmured to himself, when a voice rang out of the trees as Annabelle stepped out from under the branches.

"You taken to following women now, Trace Cassidy?" Annabelle said tartly.

She stood on the eaves of the wood, and he was once again struck by how much she had grown in the five short years since he had seen her last. She was certainly no mere girl anymore.

51

"No! Of course not. This was my place, once—how was I supposed to know you were out here?"

"*Your* place?" Annabelle shook her long black hair. "I don't see the great Cassidy name written all over it!"

Trace blinked, as if struck. Is that what this was? Was she jealous?

Then again—Trace remembered. *Yeah.* People got funny after losing loved ones. He had seen it in the war plenty of times. Heaven alone knew that he had...

The memory of kneeling in the cold and wet earth, begging for God's guidance, came back to him. He just wanted to be the sort of man his pa would have respected. He figured that maybe Annabelle had a right to be at least a little bit jealous. After all, he was the one who still had a family member. And he had the Daggers.

"Look, Annie—"

"It's *Annabelle.* Always was," she said tartly.

Trace started again. "I'm sorry about what happened to you. Truly, I am."

Annabelle swung him a sharp look as she untied her horse. Her movements were quick, fierce, angry. She'd always had a cat's temper on her, he recalled.

"Then maybe you can see what's right in front of your face, Trace. Stop being so blind. The Rattler's back!" Annabelle said in a snarl before vaulting onto her horse, and with a wheel, leapt into a canter towards the Flint residence.

He can't be! Trace bit down on the words. He took off his hat and batted some of the trail dust off his shirt. The Rattler simply couldn't be back—because that would mean that all those years of searching had been a failure. It meant that, when he went off to war, he had been endangering what little family he had left!

What would Pa do? Whatever was happening to his town, it was clear that Annabelle was shaken up, and there was danger in the air. Trace knew exactly what he had to do.

"Pa would do his best to look after his people," Trace murmured. And right now, for Trace, that meant Frankie and Sawyer and Harlan—and Annabelle, too.

It wouldn't hurt so much to go and have a word with Sheriff Jackson tomorrow.

Chapter Six

Colorado City, 1866

Colorado City wasn't exactly a peaceful place at the best of times, but right now it was a damn *powder keg.*

Trace clicked his horse to a slow trot as he hit Main Street. He kept his hat down, and his eyes slid up and down the boardwalks on either side. The air was tense. Trace could see it in the way shopkeepers stepped out, checked the street, and brought their tables inside. The grocer even pulled his wooden shutters over his windows, despite still being open.

"Yeah, I've seen this before..." Trace murmured to no one but his horse. It had been like this during the war. His unit would ride into a supposedly 'friendly' town to find the locals wary, suspicious, and paranoid.

The back of his teeth itched, and Trace couldn't help the feeling he was being watched. There was a sudden bang as someone slammed a window shut.

"You expecting trouble, mister?" Trace nodded toward an old-timer sitting on a stool outside one of the saloons. It was still early yet, but it looked like the whiskery man with a cane in one hand and a glass in the other had already taken to the drink.

"There's always trouble in Colorado City, son." The man scowled and spat, before taking a further, assessing look at Trace, up and down. "You on your own?"

Huh. The man clearly thought *he* was trouble!

"Just me and my mare, hooo." Trace said. There was a jangle of a harness as a wagon turned onto the street, laden down with baskets and leather storage cases and bags. From the looks of it, an entire family was moving out of the city, and doing so early.

"Ah, that'll be the Johnsons. Second family this week," the old-timer sighed, and took the final swig of whatever was in his tumbler. He didn't appear too happy at that, as he peered into the bottom of the glass for a long time.

"They leaving because of the war?" Trace said. The war was over. But the land was awash with deserters and de-camped soldiers. He'd heard it said that many were leaving for blue states, where there was supposed to be more money.

"You think the general's war means squat to the people out here? Naw—people got more *present* troubles to think about, young man!" the man hawed; it was somewhere between scorn and mockery.

As if the man was psychic, there was a sudden smash of broken glass, and a clamor of voices from the next street over. Trace felt his blood rise, and his hand moved to his belt at once, an old soldier's habit—just before the sound of shouting, and the gunshot.

"Aii!"

"Stop them!"

Trace hissed in frustration, tapping his feet to urge his brown chestnut mare to break into a run. His gun was up in his free hand as he rounded the street corner to see a crowd of people breaking apart outside Moat's General Store.

"Moat's!" Trace hissed. Moat's had been there since he was a kid. It was one of Pa and Sawyer's go-to places when they absolutely had to get supplies from the city.

"They shot him!" A woman's voice screamed, and Trace saw Elspeth Moat herself, the shopkeeper's sister, wearing a dark blue dress and a white apron, running out onto the boardwalk. The crowd scattered, running towards Trace, where he reared at the end of the street—and shouting in alarm when they saw him.

"No—it's not me!" Trace cried out tersely. Some of the townsfolk ran past him. Others skidded to a halt. Trace saw riders on the far side, riding away from the scene of the crime.

"Out of the way, I can't see!" His horse reared, and the last of the townsfolk jumped out of the way as Trace urged his steed forward.

"Is that them, ma'am?" Trace skidded as he pranced in front of Moat's, to see the older Elspeth looking distraught, first with fear directed at Trace himself—and then her mouth dropped open in surprise.

"Trace Cassidy?"

The widowed sister of the store owner had been living up in Denver for most of Trace's childhood, but must have come back to help her brother with the shop.

"Ma'am." Trace's voice was quick. He gestured with his gun towards the cloud of dust disappearing at the end of the street. The riders were already gone; they had started galloping, and they would be out of the city limits in a heartbeat.

"That was them, Trace—but there's too many of them. There's gotta be seven or more. I couldn't count."

"Yes, ma'am." Trace ignored her concerns, wheeling his horse and kneeing her into action. The horse flung itself forward with a sharp, controlled snort, and Trace leaned low over the chestnut's neck.

Hooves thundered. The last of the wooden two-story houses shot past, and Trace was passing the larger warehouses and granary stores after the fast-moving riders, throwing up dust ahead.

"Five. Six. Seven. Eight." Trace hissed their number as he saw them veer onto the open plains, and then whooped as they settled in for a fast, maniacal ride.

"Heading north, north–east." He muttered the words because that fixed them in his mind—an old scouting technique. They were already too far ahead for him to catch up with them, and yes, Elspeth Moat had been right when she said eight was too many to take on single-handedly.

But at least they would know that they couldn't get away unchallenged. Trace eased his steed into a slower canter, firing a couple of shots into the air to make his point clear before coming to a stop.

The gang didn't slow, and it didn't look as though they even turned around, but Trace figured they must have heard his gunshot.

He waited, keeping a sharp eye on them until they were nothing but a distant haze on the horizon, then he turned his horse back to Colorado City.

The street was in uproar by the time he arrived back, and he saw pot-bellied Sheriff Jackson with two deputies, both of whom looked ten years older than even Mr. Moat had been.

"He's dead?" Trace saw the doctor's carriage sitting outside Moat's General Store and the unhurried way that Doctor Kilgore closed the doors.

"Trace." Sheriff Jackson greeted him with a touch to his hat. Once upon a time, the man might have been impressive—as large as a bear and with as black a beard to match. But years of local home-brew had softened his bulk. His jacket and shirt strained around him, and his beard and hair were shot through with silver.

"Mighty glad a man like you is back," Jackson said in his clipped, guttural accent. "You uh, you catch sight of them?"

Trace blinked a little. The last time he had seen Sheriff Jackson, he had been nothing but a boy. Now it seemed the man saw him not as old man Cassidy's eldest kid...but as a man.

"Eight of them. Armed with revolvers, not rifles. Never seen them before. Too far away to read faces." Trace announced this like he was reporting to Captain Cooper. Jackson frowned, like he wasn't sure what to do with this information, and then sighed heavily as he took out a large white handkerchief and dabbed at the sweat on his ruddy face.

"Like I say, mighty glad you're back, Trace..." he muttered again. The deputies were talking with Elspeth and trying to set the general store straight; it looked like the men had gotten into an argument before they had decided to shoot bullets instead of throwing words.

"Truth is, we're run ragged right now. There's fights going on in the city, but there's always been those, hasn't there? But we've had word of new people moving into town. Hard people, if you catch my drift. We got ranch fires, cattle thefts..." Jackson shook his head like he was merely talking about a funeral, rather than an active battle.

"It could be we've got the attention of multiple gangs. One group is supposed to be almost a dozen strong!"

Ex-soldiers. Trace thought about some of the men he had seen disembarking on his journey back, even some of the very men who had taken the carriage with him. They had nothing left to lose and had come to Colorado City because, well, everyone knew the city was where you could get rich, right? If you were *very* lucky.

Or if you were willing to take what wasn't yours.

Trace shielded his eyes against the beat of the sun and suppressed a growl. *What does a soldier do when he's seen what he's seen? When everything he has ever loved has been taken from him?*

What did I do? Memories of that Virginia night near Bealeton blossomed in his mind, and Trace pushed them down just as quickly.

Jackson shifted in front of him and huffed uncomfortably. "Y'know, some folks are saying *he's* back."

Him. Trace knew exactly who the sheriff meant. He shook his head.

"The Rattler's gone, Sheriff." Trace's voice was tight. He felt his heart fluttering with something darker than anger. "I searched for him, Jackson. For years after. And I found nothing."

The sheriff sighed once more. "I know you did, Trace, I know you did. But people are scared."

Trace bit his tongue, in case he told the sheriff to do his job better. It was clear that the man knew nothing about what was going on, and the best place to get information was always directly from the townsfolk and ranchers themselves.

Of course, the Rattler wasn't back. Trace fumed as he thanked the sheriff and passed his respects to Elspeth, before leading his horse around the block and stopping at Leary's All-Star Saloon. It was perhaps one of the roughest of the drinking dens in Colorado City, and Trace had always been expressly forbidden to go in.

But what if it was true? What if the Rattler was back? It was almost too much for Trace to consider, and as if to prove it to himself, he decided to find out. He knew what the Rattler looked like. The cultured, baritone growl of the man still haunted his dreams sometimes.

"And those darn fancy leather red gloves of his!" Trace muttered angrily as he fixed his horse to the post outside and walked in to find the saloon full of noise and chaos.

Word of Mr. Moat's death had already spread like wildfire, it seemed, but most of the folks here were people that Trace didn't know from Adam. Had Colorado City's population swelled that much?

Leary's All Star was little more than two long, interconnecting rooms, with a bar running down the wall of one. The air was heavy with cigar smoke and the smell of stale beer. Teamsters and ranch hands mixed freely, talking loudly with surly, rough-looking men with guns on their hips. Trace figured that not a small number of them were ex-soldiers, but it was impossible to tell from which side.

"Hey, Trace!"

It was Harlan, signaling to him from where he sat by the window.

"Just like old times?" Harlan called for another round and shot Trace a tired grin. Despite the parental prohibition, there had been at least a couple of times that the younger Harlan and Trace had sneaked into Leary's—and then there was the time Harlan had dragged him out, after the fire.

"Hopefully not," Trace said, accepting the shot of rye from the pretty saloon girl he didn't know. "A lot of new faces around here these days." He looked over his drink at the assembled numbers around them.

"Started happening halfway through the war," Harlan nodded. "Rough sorts, more than a few runaways, I think. Some stuck, most of them carried on west. Now there's a steady turnover."

"You think that's what is going on around here? Soldiers?" Trace asked. Harlan caught what he meant at once. He leaned over the table and kept his voice low.

"Most, but not all. I've spent this last year trying to track them. I'm starting to guess there might be *two* gangs out there, and they're warring for territory. Our territory," he whispered.

Trace nodded sharply, keeping an eye on the crowd. There was so much liquor flowing around that it didn't look as though anyone had even noticed them.

"I've overheard people talking about meetings. And trouble, out on the prairies. But every time I try to get closer, ask if I can join maybe—they clam up." Harlan scowled. He took another sip of his drink and then thumped his chest. The stuff they brewed at Leary's was strong enough to strip tar.

"But it's bad, Trace. Real bad," Harlan said after he got his voice back. "I don't know if Frankie told you everything that happened to the Flints..."

Trace winced. "Some." In truth, he still felt bad about that. Annabelle was hurting, and he should have been there for her.

"They took everyone. Fired the barn to lure them out, and then went on a shooting spree." Harlan shivered. "Pa and I rode over with Sheriff Jackson and a few others to clean up. She was darn lucky that they never torched the house...but they took *everything* else."

His friend's voice was heavy, wary, as if he were stalking around something.

"Frankie said the gang...that they might have held her?" Trace forced himself to ask.

Harlan's eyes shot to his quickly, a look of horror on his face before he shook his head. "Not long. My father got me when he saw the smoke, so it must have only been an hour at most, but..."

Sometimes an hour lasts a lifetime. Trace felt a shiver run over his body. How long had it taken from moving between Wade and Cole being alive and well and annoying, to being cold on the dirt?

A tremor ran through Trace's hands, so much so that he had to set down the tumbler. It wasn't shock. It was an anger so deep that he swore it came up from the bowels of hell itself.

But instead of heat and flames, a terrible cold settled on Trace. He even felt light-headed.

"You got any descriptions of the gangs? Their leader?" Trace asked. He would need descriptions if he was going to put an end to them, and there was only one detail he didn't want to hear. Red gloves.

Before Harlan could get to it, however, there was a smash of glass and a sudden shout from behind him.

"You miserable yeller-belly! You ain't got no business being in Colorado City!"

Trace and Harlan spun around just as the first fist flew, and the smaller man went flying. As Trace and Harlan leapt to their feet, the man's friends were already flying forwards with fists and boots, and roars of outrage joined them.

"Oh darn it!" Harlan snapped. "I can't see what started it!"

"It doesn't matter what started it!" Trace yelled, dodging as a stool came flying towards him to bounce off the wall. "Someone's going to pull a gun before long!"

Colorado City was a powder keg, alright, and Trace reckoned that it was just about to blow.

He whipped out his pistol and fired, one shot, straight into the ceiling. At the deafening sound, there were shouts and a couple of screams, but it had the desired effect as people scrabbled away from him.

"Break it up! We're not doing this in *my* town!" Trace yelled, stalking forward with his gun at his side as he glared at everyone who dared to look at him. Harlan followed him a pace behind.

"*Your* town?" someone sneered.

"That's right!" Trace spun around, and a wave of low moans and scrabbling feet followed him as everyone struggled to get away from his revolver's baleful attention.

Any one of these men could be from the gang that killed Mr. Moats. Or... the gang that attacked Annabelle, he thought.

"That's right. This is *my* town. I live here. I grew up here. I spilled blood for this soil!" Trace snarled. The crowd went silent. He saw a whole lot of angry, shocked, and scared eyes.

Trace eased a little. His shoulders dropped, but he kept his gun up. "You lot want to ease off. A *lot*. I know things are bad, and we're going through some trials—but this fighting and hollering won't do you any favors, believe me." Trace wasn't sure if his last words were a promise or a threat, as he glared around the room one more time before he nodded to the barman and sauntered out.

Trace and Harlan walked quickly, keeping an eye behind them just in case any of the irate drinkers decided to test their resolve once again, but none of them did. Trace took a deep, shuddering breath and realized that this entire city smelled like stale alcohol. He hated it here and yearned for the purple and green prairies.

Beside him, Harlan looked just as concerned and agitated about the events of the day. First, Mr. Moat's murder, now this fight.

"You see what it's like, Trace. People are on edge. I swear that none of this is going to end well," Harlan said glumly—and Trace thought he might agree.

Chapter Seven

Flint Ranch, 1866

"No ma'am, it would be silly to buy extra feed right now; you have months until winter," the ranch hand, a good-looking young man named Valentin, rolled his eyes and put a hand on his hip.

He spoke the words loudly for the audience of Annabelle's two other ranch hands leaning on the yard gate behind him, who chuckled.

How dare he! Annabelle did her best to not scream at the man. They were about the same age, but the ranch hand smirked at her as if she was a fool. It had been like this ever since her parents had died, and Annabelle had relied on Valentin and the other ranch hands a whole lot more in the running of the ranch.

"But *now* is the time that the feed prices are cheap, Valentin. And grain will keep. So that's why I asked you to go to the granary today—but you didn't!" Annabelle said.

Valentin looked back at the others pointedly, reacting like she was hysterical.

"This is how we have always done it, Ms. Flint. How we have done it since your father, rest his soul, was in charge."

Annabelle felt her hands clench at her sides. "Don't talk about my father!"

Good-looking, dark-haired Valentin looked at her with a grin like he had won something.

Did he WANT me to look hysterical in front of his friends? Is that what he thinks this is? That I am just some fool woman? Annabelle fumed.

"Ms. Annabelle, please, I know that all of this land, and all of these animals can be a lot to think about—" Valentin started to say. He even added small, placating gestures with his hands as he said it, as if she were a bucking stallion. Behind him, the two other ranch hands turned away so she wouldn't see their laughter.

Annabelle shook with rage, but before she could put voice to her words, Valentin was speaking.

"Look, Ms. Annabelle. There is something else which is very important, and that is our pay. The times are very uncertain right now, ranches are getting attacked all over. We think that we should be paid early," Valentin said a little more seriously. "This is dangerous work, after all."

"You don't get paid until the end of the month! You know this, Valentin. It's always been like this." Annabelle spluttered.

"Yes, but with more attacks now, and you saying you want to spend ranch stores buying new winter grain, it makes me think..." Valentin started to say.

"Makes you think what, Valentin?" Annabelle shot at him.

The man's once charming face revealed its true glower of discontent. "If you cannot pay us, then there are other, better-run ranches that can," the man said.

Oh really? "All of the ranches are suffering attacks, Valentin," Annabelle said coldly. "But you are free to try your hand elsewhere if you don't like how I run things here. Or if you can't agree!" She dared them.

"Bah!" Valentin shouted, kicking the dirt and stalking away, speaking rapidly to the other ranch hands as they marched back towards their bunkhouse.

Annabelle watched them go for a moment, and then, realizing that she was just working herself up even more, she turned and stalked to the stables herself, selecting Constance.

I have to get some fresh air. Frankie's.

Frankie had always been as close as a sister to Annabelle through all their time growing up.

"And I guess she's the only sister I have right now." Her thoughts turned dark as she saddled and mounted the white-and-black horse, and set off for the Cassidy ranch.

The Cassidys were good people. Annabelle knew that, of course. Their families had been raised together after all.

But then there was Trace Cassidy.

She felt a flicker of hot annoyance as the steady rhythm of Constance's hooves ate up the sage-lands turned greener around her, and white clouds scudded high overhead.

"He was always a dunderhead," Annabelle admitted to Constance, who snorted as she cantered.

Trace was maddening. But he hadn't always been, had he? When she tried to put her finger on exactly what was so wrong with him, all she could come up with was a vague sense of loss.

Trace Cassidy was the oldest in their group. The group that had once contained her, Trace, Frankie, Harlan, Cole, Garret and Kaylee, and Wade... A hand of ice clutched at her heart, and Annabelle drew her breath. Of course, most of their group was now gone.

Was that what this was? Whenever she thought of Trace, she thought of the older, wilder boy he had been. Always the first to find the adder's nest or to jump into the creek. Did she miss the way he was—and what they had all been together?

"I know he can be strong," she admitted to herself. And yes, she did miss what they had when they'd all been together. She yearned for some of the old Trace's reckless bravery right now, his total loyalty to his family and friends.

She arrived at the Cassidy ranch to see a little smoke coming from the chimney, and to hear the sound of clattering pots from the open door to the kitchen. A second later, and the smell of fresh baking, sweet and yeasty, made her stomach grumble.

"Who's that?" Frankie's sharp yell came from the side of the house, and before Annabelle could raise her voice, light-haired Frankie appeared at her kitchen step, armed with a rather large iron pot and a fierce glare.

"Oh, it's you. Gracious. You scared the life out of me," she laughed as soon as she saw who it was.

"Sorry. Is this a bad time? I just needed..." Annabelle's voice trailed off. She had already dismounted and tied Constance to the rail outside, but looked hesitantly back at her horse. Maybe she had already asked too much of the Cassidys, and now that Trace was back...

"Oh, don't be silly. It's never a bad time for you. You know that," Frankie said, ushering her into the kitchen where Annabelle was immediately wrapped in the rich aroma of baking and coffee.

"I just put a tray on, as Trace and Harlan should be back soon." Frankie returned the iron pot to its hook above the stove and turned to inspect Annabelle. "You alright? Has anything happened?"

"Well—I may have just lost my ranch hands." Annabelle shrugged and proceeded to tell Frankie everything that had happened that morning, from Valentin and the others routinely disrespecting her because she was 'just a woman' to now getting cold feet because of the attacks.

"But the attacks affect everyone! There isn't a ranch around here they can find work at where that won't be the case," Frankie burst out.

"I know. That's what I said." Annabelle sighed, and for a moment, stared at the unpoured coffee, lost in her thoughts.

"You'll get through this, Annabelle." Frankie crossed over and quickly pressed her hand to Annabelle's own, giving it a squeeze before pouring two small cups of thick, strong coffee. "I can ask Sawyer and Harlan to stop over at yours. I'm sure they'll say yes. And, to be honest, now that Trace is back, he can take on a greater share of the ranch work around here…"

"Trace," Annabelle said a little carefully. She saw Frankie's eyes flicker to hers warily.

Yeah, I guess we did have a blow-out the last time we saw each other.

"How is that going? Him being back?" Annabelle said a little stiffly.

Frankie rolled her eyes. "Oh, he's Trace! What do you expect? He barely says a word to me in the morning, grumbles about this and every other thing, and then tries to fix everything all on his own!" She laughed at that before sobering. "He's just like Pa in that."

It was Annabelle's turn to reach out and take a hold of her friend's hand as Frankie sat down.

"He's still in there, Annabelle. I know he is. But the war...I think it affected him more than he lets on. He hasn't told me one word about what happened yet." Frankie's smile was sad.

"Of course," Annabelle said, and instantly felt a blush of shame rise to her cheeks. Trace had lost his own baby brother too, right before his eyes, hadn't he?

In that, we have a lot in common...

"But in better news," Frankie cleared her throat, shaking her head as if she could shake all of the bad memories away.

It's impossible. Believe me, I've tried.

"Harlan," Frankie said purposefully and raised her eyebrows.

"Harlan?" Annabelle asked, before realizing. "Oh. I thought you two were getting close over the last few years."

"Well," her friend laughed again, and Annabelle saw how pretty she was. Harlan would be a fool not to choose her.

"I loved Cole, I really did—still *do*," Frankie said with certainty. She was nervous, and Annabelle could tell she was eager for her opinion, maybe her blessing.

"Of course," Annabelle murmured.

"But I've been noticing Harlan for a while—the way he speaks to me, or gets nervous around me—the little things, you know?" Frankie blushed deeply. "Well...I think he's going to ask me to marry him."

"You should," Annabelle said at once.

"You think?" Frankie appeared surprised. "But—you don't think it's too soon after...?"

Annabelle fixed her friend with a serious stare. "Look, Frankie. We've always been honest with each other, haven't we?"

"Always." Her friend nodded.

"Then listen up. If you think that there's anything in you that's sweet on Harlan, that can see a life for you together—then take that opportunity. Life is too short," Annabelle said.

Frankie looked about to answer, but before she could—there was a shout from the yard.

"Annabelle! You got Annabelle in there with you, Frankie?" It was Sawyer, riding in hard to pull up suddenly, his horse's hooves kicking up dust.

"Sawyer! What on earth is going on?" Frankie cried out. Both women ran to the yard to see that Sawyer was catching his breath and gesturing back out southwest.

Back towards my ranch.

"There's a barn fire at your place, Annabelle. I saw it checking the stock, and I've been searching for you ever since. Thank God you're safe," he gasped.

Annabelle felt like she had been struck by a bullet. Another fire. Just like last time.

It was all happening again, wasn't it?

Chapter Eight

Western Colorado Territories, 1866

So much...uncertainty. Axel Bishop looked out of a window that wasn't his, on a ranch that he didn't own, and didn't like what he saw.

The gold and green plains gave themselves up to the stamp of the Colorado mountains easily, and right now, a fierce wind was bringing clouds piling up over the mountains. If he was any judge, that would turn into a storm by tonight.

The ranch he was on was small and old, tucked into the folds of hills, and had belonged to a prospector-turned-homesteader who had been easy to intimidate. It's amazing what a man is willing to give up if you put a gun to his head.

"No staying power. No...*legacy.*" Axel pulled a face.

To him, the only enduring thing he could see out there was the mountains, or the rise of the storm—still a long way off yet—itself.

"Everything here will go, in time. This ranch. Even that darn town. Nothing...*endures.*" The broad, barrel-chested man grunted.

"Boss?" There was a cough behind him, as Briggs, his right-hand man, had stepped into the room apparently without Axel noticing.

"Why didn't you knock?" Axel turned with a roar. He could still summon the thunder when he needed to. Briggs was no weakling—he stood six foot if he stood an inch, and had weathered features, his skin reddened with the sun and short, light brown hair. Not a lot quailed him, but Axel was pleased with the look of alarm that crossed the younger man's face.

"I—I did knock, sir, several times," Briggs said.

"*Pfagh!*" Axel snarled. "Clearly not loud enough then. What are you, a mouse?"

He saw Briggs splutter a bit, the anger coming too fast for the man to do anything about it. This kind of dominance was almost too easy for Axel. It was like he could see exactly what people were sometimes. He could see the animal in them—knew when they were going to fold, or when they were going to break. He didn't think it was a skill he was born with, but one he had learned.

One he *had* to learn.

"Spit it out. Why are you here, disturbing my rest!" Axel snapped. He walked away from the window to plump himself down on the fine chair, molded to curve around his back. It was the nicest thing in this dump of a hideout, he had to admit.

"Moat's," Briggs said, even standing a little straighter like he was back in his abortive army days.

"Moat's?" Axel's brain went first to watery defenses. Was that Briggs's plan? What a ridiculous idea! This hideout was well hidden, and by now, nearly everyone who had ever seen his face had either died in the war or was too scared to even recall it in dreams.

"Moat's General Store. Clay took his men and killed the old man just this morning," Briggs said.

"Clay Slade." Axel leered at the name, rolling it around his tongue and spitting it like the last dreg of bitter, chewed tobacco.

73

"Idiot!" Axel hissed with such vehemence that it caused Briggs to take a half step backwards.

"That man is wet behind the ears, and he has no *idea* what he is doing! He's only going to provoke Colorado City to get antsy and reach for their guns as soon as spit!" Axel snarled.

Clay Slade and his gang of young bucks were making things difficult. Ever since they had arrived last year, the band of mostly ex-soldiers and deserters had done nothing *clever.* They hadn't picked on the post wagons coming in, or isolated the officials, or selected the weakest ranches.

No—Clay Slade and his wild men were still drunk on gunpowder and were attacking anything and everyone, willy-nilly.

Axel drew himself up and pulled his embroidered, deep red waistcoat a tad tighter over his muscled bulk. He liked to think that he knew better—*no*—he knew that he knew better. He hadn't survived being the leader of the most successful gang across the entire Western Colorado territory by being as stupid as Clay Slade was.

At first, Axel had thought that Clay was going to go the way that most young blowhards did. In a hail of bullets, as they picked the wrong ranch with the right number of friends. That's how the young outlaws usually went, or they bit off more than they could chew and ended up calling down the attention of the U.S. Marshals or even—God forbid—the nearest U.S. army.

Axel had even thought that a few well-placed threats of his own, making it clear that the city was *his* and *his* alone, should have sent the message loud and clear.

After all—who dared take on the Rattler on his home turf? Who would be so stupid, or so monumentally suicidal?

The most outrageous thing was that Clay Slade had managed to survive. And his ranks kept on swelling as washed-up soldiers, their blood still roaring with battle lust and cheap rye. There was no end to what Axel saw as an endless procession of damned, wild, and hopeless men. They found Colorado City like ticks found a steer in open country—lured by the promise of the gold rush, and being broken just as quickly because of it.

Some of those damned men soon lost all their money and whatever wits they had left in the city's saloons, brothels, and opium dens. They started fights and were either gunned down on the street or washed away, heading to Denver or even further west, to the large, evergreen promised land of California territory.

And it was these very people that Clay Slade recruited. No wonder they had no respect.

"No attention to *legacy*." Axel glowered, his eyes once again flicking to the window and the immovable, eternal hills outside.

"Boss?" Briggs asked, sounding confused.

Axel spun on him, anger flaring. Why was Briggs himself so slow-witted sometimes? What was it with everyone?

"Briggs. I know this is going to be hard to follow, but there is something you have to understand if you are to achieve in this life," Axel said.

Just like Pa used to say. The thought made the Rattler feel uncomfortable. His father had never respected him. Had always demanded more of him. Had always preached about doing what was 'right' and 'true' and never actually did *anything* to stop the men who came and took his life, and that of his wife, and—almost—all of his children.

"Boss." Briggs' answer wasn't a question this time, although he did still look confused.

"It's about legacy. That's what you young fellas don't understand. That's what a whippersnapper like Clay Slade doesn't understand."

"*Boss?*" Briggs looked positively challenged. "I thought it was about making as much money as we could—"

"*DID I TELL YOU TO SPEAK?*" Axel suddenly roared, smashing his heavy fist on his desk with such force that his ink jar jumped and spilled. Briggs looked suitably chastised and shuffled his feet.

Axel drew the moment out longer, waiting for his lieutenant's discomfort to grow and grow until...

"I took over this area, Briggs, by being ruthless. But also by being clever," the Rattler announced, like he was giving a speech in a town hall. Just like the sorts of speeches his own pa used to make.

"We take out the weak ranches first. We offer them the opportunity to hand over their claims to me, and if they don't, we persuade them," Axel grinned slowly. "And if they prove difficult, we destroy them."

He stalked around the desk, pacing before the window. "My name is feared under these halls. There are women who tuck their children into bed at night, praying that the Rattler doesn't come for them while they sleep. You get that sort of respect by being consistent and by following through on your promises. Not by random, stupid attacks on general store keepers!"

In Axel's mind, he could see the shining path ahead of him.

There was a chance here, and Axel could almost taste it. Colorado territory was about to be recognized—everyone with any eyes could see that, Kansas State would cede its claim to western Colorado, and everything from the plains to the mountains and right to the edge of California itself would become its own state.

But who would govern it? Who would control it—that was the question.

Surely a man like the Rattler, with his standing and his power, had a chance?

"But I need a wife," Axel said, his mind skipping to the next part of the problem, while Briggs was clearly struggling to catch up.

"All good rulers have a wife. A first family. A unit that everyone looks up to, that sets the example!" Axel turned around to see that Briggs looked shocked.

Poor man. He really hasn't got the brains for this, has he? Axel felt almost sorry for him.

"The woman. The one who got away," Axel said.

"Annabelle Flint, Boss?" Briggs struggled. "You want us to get Annabelle Flint for you?"

Yes. Annabelle Flint. Even the name sent shivers down Axel's spine. She was attractive in a way that a wild cougar was. Or a hunting hawk, screaming towards its prey. Axel didn't think he had seen anything like her. He had to admit that his thoughts turned to her often.

"Yes. I will have her. You did as I asked?" Axel said.

Briggs nodded at once. "We set fire to her barn, and now we have word that her ranch hands have left. She can't have much money left, so she should be ready to make a deal on her land."

"She will make a deal with *me*," Axel insisted, almost purring at the thought.

There was a moment of silence, in which Briggs looked distinctly uncomfortable. "Boss?" he said after a moment.

"What?"

"It's uh—Clay. The people in Colorado City are blaming you for the attack. They don't know that there's another gang out there."

Axel bared his teeth like a dog. Of course, Clay would do that. The young pup was scratching to start a war, wasn't he?

Well, if he wanted a war, then he could have one!

"And there's something else, Boss. One of our men saw someone in the city. Someone we haven't seen for a long time. The Cassidy boy. Only, he's not a boy any more. He's a man. He's come back from the war and looks mean... looks... capable," Briggs said.

"Trace Cassidy," Axel remembered the name. So. The time had come to settle that particular problem as well, had it? It looked like he was about to have a very busy summer ahead of him.

The Rattler grinned.

Chapter Nine

Cassidy Ranch, 1866

But why would the Rattler take out Mr. Moat now, of all times? Trace thought as he rode at a steady clip over the prairie lands. Even the steady, fresh breeze and the sight of the rolling hills around him weren't helping to ease his worried mind.

Harlan, too, who rode a little behind him, seemed to be as lost in thought as he was.

Mr. Moat had been a fixture of Colorado City for about as long as anyone could remember. Certainly, since Trace was a kid. He was irritable, and he was firm—but he was always fair. It was that quality that made him respected by the homesteaders around the city, like the Cassidys and the Flints.

"It sends a signal," Trace murmured to himself. It said to the entire city that the Rattler could reach in and take whoever he wanted, whenever he wanted.

But there was something else, something deeper, that was bothering him.

"Why now?"

"Trace?" Harlan pulled up alongside him, clearly hearing him mumble.

Trace slowed into a walk and admitted to the confusion he had. "Something about it just doesn't make sense. The Rattler was always a ghost. He came in the night, attacked—and then was gone the next day. It was the whole reason why it was so difficult to track him down...and difficult for my pa and Mr. Flint, back in the day."

Trace looked back now on the half-overheard conversations between Pa and the Flint patriarch and thought he understood them a lot better. The two men had been trying to rally the city to do something about the Rattler, and they had failed. Colorado City was just as bad back then as it was now, and Sheriff Jackson had never exactly been inspiring.

And, in the end, everyone knew that the Rattler attacked those who dared stand up to him. That was what had happened to the Cassidys and the Flints, wasn't it?

"He's an outlaw. What reason do they have for anything?" Harlan pointed out. "All they care about is destruction and money."

Trace nodded at that. He had seen a fair few people like that during the war, too. Seeing death did something to a man, sometimes. It either made you cruel or it made you strong.

Trace hoped he had come out of it the right way, and not the other.

"True. But the Rattler was always smart," Trace said. "He always killed for a reason. Whether it was to get rid of an obstacle or to move a family off a claim, right? What reason is there to kill Mr. Moat? His sister has still got the business. All it does is get everyone riled up in town. He's twice as likely to have people ready to draw guns on him now than before."

Yeah, Trace couldn't see the sense of it. But then again, maybe Harlan was right and he was just trying to make reason where there was none.

'Young pup.'

The long ago words of the bandit outlaw came back, and with them came the smell of smoke, and the echo of screams. Trace had shot him, and he had only grunted like it was nothing but a scratch. The outlaw had even laughed at him. What did a man like that have to fear from a grocer?

Smoke.

Trace blinked. The smell of smoke wasn't just in his mind. It was—*it was here!*

"Harlan!" he suddenly hissed, raising his head to point over his friend's shoulder, to where a billow of dark smoke was rising on the horizon, out north-west, right up against the Calico Pass.

"That's the Flints' place! Annabelle!" Trace burst out, immediately surging into a gallop as he raced across the prairies.

It was happening again. It was all happening again.

Annabelle! Trace's heart twitched in his chest as he pushed his steed to go faster. But with every long, lunging reach of his horse's legs, he didn't feel nearer; he felt like he was running out of precious time.

"Up ahead! I see Father!" Harlan shouted, as they rode up rising land, to where the Flint ranch sat straddling the brow of a hill, its meadows and cattle lands rolling behind it. The smoke had turned an ugly black now, and Trace could see that the flames had taken one wall of their new barn. There were even embers starting to fly to the main house, too.

There were figures before the flames, too, as Trace saw Frankie and Sawyer—and then Annabelle herself running forwards with a bucket to throw it at the base of the flames.

Too close! Trace's heart leapt to his throat. Annabelle's black hair was streaming behind her, and she was fearless in trying to save her building. She ducked close, almost into the flames, to throw her precious water before jumping back.

Sawyer and Frankie were both running back and forth to the well as quickly as they could, and Trace saw at once how it was causing problems as Frankie and Annabelle were the quickest—but they had to wait to winch water.

He skidded his horse in the yard and jumped off, slapping her rear to know that she would run to seek safety away from the flames without him having to guide her.

And Trace saw what he had to do at once.

"Harlan, with me to the winch!" He shouted in a voice he thought he had left behind him in the war.

The two young men moved as one, running past the others as Frankie and Sawyer called out to them. Their feet skidded as they got to the well.

The Flint well was a simple bucket-and-drop design, with a bar and a winch that you could use to lower it more steadily. Trace grabbed the winch at once.

"Throw bucket, haul," Trace said, grabbing the only empty bucket left, slipping its handle over the hook and then spinning the winch with all of his might. It spun, blurring for a moment until there was a sudden splash underneath them. Trace caught the chaotic winch and set to powering it back up as Sawyer ran up, panting.

"Harlan, Trace, am I darn pleased to see you! The fire must have started this morning. By the time we got here, it was already steady."

Trace eyed him as he raised the bucket back up to the surface. Frankie was already running back behind the older man, who was panting for air.

Too slow.

"Sawyer? Can you find more buckets? Pots? Try the Flint kitchen, stores, and pantry." Trace said the old man responded like he had just been given a military command, and set off at once.

The bucket got to the top, and Trace thumped it in front of Harlan, before grabbing the next from Frankie, slipping it on the hook, and repeating the process. He knew he could keep this pace for a bit yet; he still hadn't even broken into the reserves of stamina that every soldier developed.

Harlan passed Annabelle, and as soon as Trace had thumped a bucket into his sister's hands, Annabelle was next at his side.

"Trace..." she said, shocked for a moment. "Thank you."

Trace didn't bat an eyelid. "Don't mention it." This is what you did for neighbors, didn't you?

Annabelle looked about to say something else, but then grabbed the bucket of water and ran. He had filled the next by the time Harlan returned, and the system started working. Trace's shoulders ached, and he felt the smoke worrying his eyes, but he pushed on. He could be meaner than this fire. He knew it.

"Trace!" It was Sawyer, skidding on the dirt with pots on his hand, and pointing up to the roof of the main Flint ranch house.

Oh no. Trace followed the older man's gaze to see that sparks had caught in a couple of places, and the hot, arid wind was only feeding them.

"I got this—go!" Harlan appeared at his side, grabbing the winch handle as Trace snarled in frustration. They had almost controlled the fire on the barn (although two sides of the building looked almost completely blackened).

If the fire caught on the roof, then it would be hard to keep the building, Trace knew. He turned to see Annabelle stumbling to a stop, looking up in horror at the house her parents had built.

"Ladder!" He yelled at once for Annabelle to point towards the stables.

"Rest of you keep going!" Trace yelled and broke into a run, flying across the yard and into the relative cool of the empty stables, where a long barn ladder hung sideways on the wall. He grabbed the wooden rungs, wrenched it from its position and ran back to thump it on the Flints' front porch. It was tall and reached almost to the roof itself.

"Water!" Sawyer shouted, already having filled a bucket and passing it into one of Trace's hands. The climb was awkward with the heavy pail, but Trace near ran up the ladder to lean at the top, and threw the water over the wooden shingles.

"Again!" Trace shouted, turning to throw the pail down towards the well, as Harlan thumped another pot on the ground for Sawyer to ferry to the ladder.

Trace lost count of how many times he threw water, only stopping when the wood had taken on a darker shade.

"I think we got it!" Harlan shouted behind him, for Trace to look around and see that, yes, the barn was finally out too—

but it looked a state. It would require an almost total rebuild to make sure that the framing posts were still good.

"Thank heavens," Annabelle murmured. Trace saw her stumble back to the well and slump against it, as Frankie and Sawyer joined her.

It was getting late. The fight against the fire had taken most of the afternoon, and Trace thought they would only have a couple hours of sunlight left.

"We should get back home," he said, climbing down the ladder and not realizing just how much his body ached. It happened like that, he remembered. He never felt tired or exhausted during battle, only afterwards.

"Home?" Annabelle raised her head, and she looked bereft. Her face was smeared with soot and ash, and her eyes were wide and hollow.

"Our ranch," Trace said firmly. "The Cassidy ranch. You can't stay here tonight." He paused, licked his lips, and tasted bitter, acrid char.

"In fact, you shouldn't stay here at all," he said. "Not with everything that's going on. You're going to stay with me and Frankie." He grabbed a pail of water and threw it over his head. He felt momentary relief, but it didn't last long.

"I am, am I?" Annabelle said, turning to look over her shoulder at him. There was a glimmer of her former self in that, but Trace could see that she was also exhausted. This fire had beaten her today.

But that's not tomorrow, right?

"Yes," Trace said firmly. "I'll stay and bring your horses over. But you'll be safer at ours, and it's close enough that we can keep an eye on the ranch."

"Yes! And you know we've still got that spare room." Frankie was more excited, putting an arm over her friend's shoulder where they both leaned against the stones of the well. For a moment, Trace saw through time, back to when they were all hanging out in Little Creek. Frankie used to walk with her arm on Annabelle's shoulders just like that.

The Flints and the Cassidys, always together. Trace wondered if he could hear his father's voice in that.

He saw a look of gratitude flash over Annabelle's face, but as soon as she had let herself be vulnerable, he saw her take a breath and her armor go back up. Her eyes hardened. Whatever he had thought, she was not the wild and carefree girl he had grown up with. That Annabelle was gone.

"We'll *all* get the horses. I won't have anyone else doing my work for me." She got to her feet, pausing only to wipe the soot from her face before marching to the stables.

They worked until evening, getting the horses back together and checking on the paddock gates where her cattle roamed. Trace knew that one of them would have to ride out to check on the herd tomorrow, but for now, they would be alright. The steers had sense enough to get away from the smoke as soon as they had smelled it.

They were all exhausted on the trail back, but it was one that each and every one of them knew well. Trace let his horse follow the trail back home and pulled himself back to ride beside Annabelle.

"Trace." Her hat bobbed in the gathering gloom.

"Annabelle... I'm sorry." Trace muttered. He didn't like admitting he was wrong, but he also was no oaf that ignored it. "I think the Rattler *is* back, and he clearly still wants your ranch, but I also think that there's more going on here."

He and Harlan had filled the others in on the events in Colorado City and the shooting of Mr. Moat.

"The Rattler never did stuff like that; he didn't shoot people in the middle of town. He was..." A shiver of rage ran down Trace's spine.

"Targeted." Annabelle supplied, her voice thick with rage.

"Yeah." Had he said the wrong thing? Was this the wrong time?

"It would take a lot of people." Annabelle surprised him by continuing, even though it sounded like she was talking through gritted teeth. "To ride into town, and to keep watch on my ranch. The Rattler never had the numbers for two things at once."

Trace was once again in awe at how tough she was. In fact, he would feel better if she had started crying or shouting about how unfair it was.

Because it was unfair. All of it was.

They had thought that they were finally clear of the war, and clear of the Rattler—but not so.

"I'll help you rebuild, but you stay as long as you want, until we figure this out," Trace said solemnly.

And there was only one way he could think of to figure out a problem like this. He scowled at the gathering darkness on the horizon. He would have to fight. And he was sure he was going to win.

Chapter Ten

Cassidy Ranch, 1866

Rifle. Smith & Wesson six-shooter. Bullet belt.

Trace looked at the small display of death that lay on the kitchen table before him and winced. It wasn't enough for what he knew was coming.

"But I also don't need it all today," he murmured, picking up the rifle and the bullet belt, and carefully placing them back into their oiled canvas cloth.

"Trace?" Annabelle's voice surprised him from the open kitchen door, and he turned to see her holding a basket laden with today's eggs, fresh from the chicken coop.

It had been a few days since the fire at Annabelle's ranch, and despite the many years they had known each other, Trace still saw a stiffness in her every time they talked.

Understandable, he reckoned. She'd lost all her family last year. And now her ranch had been attacked for a second time. Right now, her eyes were on the guns. Her back was straight, and Trace thought she had that same dead-eyed stare that he had seen a hundred times before on the faces of soldiers in the front lines.

"You got a lead? I'm coming too." Annabelle said at once.

"It's not like that. I just want to have a chat with some people in the city. Try to drum up some support, talk to Keeley," Trace said. He winced slightly. He hadn't told her he was going to do this, figuring she would want to recover from the shock of the attack.

"Mayor Keeley is about as much use as a fifth horseshoe." Annabelle suddenly laughed, but there was no humor in it. Trace could hear the bitterness and resentment.

"He hasn't changed then." Trace offered a weary smile and saw it echoed on Annabelle's face for just a moment before the shutters came down. Her brow lowered.

"He'll have to now."

Now... that the Rattler is back. Trace finished her silent sentence.

And Mayor Keeley? That old timer had been less use than Sheriff Jackson, Trace remembered. Keeley was a Colorado City original, his belly made fat by all the *alleged* bribes he took to look the other way from the opium dens and the less-than-legal liquor imports that supplied half the saloons.

"I'll get my things." Annabelle thumped the eggs down on the table and moved at once to strip her work shirt over her blouse, exchanging it for her dark green canvas jacket that hung by the kitchen door. She disappeared through the hallway, and a moment later returned with her own six-iron strapped to her hip.

There was no saying no to a woman like Annabelle Flint, Trace thought. Who knew? Maybe her personal testimony would help what he needed to get done.

Trace took Bella, while Annabelle had her brown saddle-bred, Prince, who Trace remembered as a wild, frisky foal. She had done a good job with him, as now the horse was steady and quiet.

"You're good with the horses. You ever thought of breeding?" Trace complimented her as they rode the green and gold prairie towards Colorado City. She'd always had a good way with the horses, he remembered. He didn't think he could remember a single time she had ever been thrown or stamped.

"Why do you say that?" Annabelle looked at him as if he had just accused her of washing her smalls in public.

Easy there, what did I say wrong?

"Father wanted a cattle ranch. That's what the Flints do," Annabelle supplied, and set her eyes on the distant haze of the city.

"Just saying." Trace felt ornery at that. Annabelle had always been a bit prickly, but now, just chatting to her was like trying to handle a porcupine.

His musings were distracted by the distant creak of wagons and the champing of horses as he saw a delivery wagon heading for the first of the Colorado City buildings. The city had grown bigger in just the few years he had been away, with actual stone buildings and pavements in the heart of town.

The city was also busy as they clipped in, with delivery carts unloading barrels at the saloons, and baker's boys on bicycles delivering hessian sacks full of today's bread. Trace saw people sitting on chairs on the porch outside of the various establishments, smoking pipes or nursing bottles—and most with six-shooters on their waist.

Yeah. Colorado City was a town of would-be gunfighters, Trace thought. Probably because some of the older ones remember the old Jefferson Free territory days, when all around here had been a free state. Trace would have thought that meant they'd be better at protecting their own...

"Jackson!" Annabelle called out when they rounded the street to see the squat, square stone building that was the sheriff's station and jail, with the sheriff himself sitting on his own porch, holding court with a couple of younger deputies.

"Miss Flint, I heard the news just this morning. I was about to send Cephas up your way to check on you..." The white-haired Sheriff Jackson struggled out of his chair, and one of his deputies—thankfully, a much younger man, who was built like a bull—turned to touch the brim of his hat.

"No need. I'm here now." Annabelle barely kept the scorn from her lips.

"Well, come in, come in. I'll take your account, and uh..." Jackson's voice wavered just a little after that, as if he was unsure of quite what he had the power to do.

"Form a posse," Trace broke in. He tipped his hat to the sheriff and Deputy Cephas. "It's the only way, Sheriff. We need a group of men willing to protect the city and the homesteaders."

"Well, uh, yes. I've already asked for some more deputies." Jackson blinked a little. His eyes were rheumy, and Trace wondered if he could still even see clearly enough to shoot straight.

"How about the U.S. Marshals up at Fort Weld?" Trace asked. Jackson blinked, a look of irritation crossing his face.

"Trace, well, y'know no one down here likes to involve the Federal Army if we don't have to."

"Fair." Trace shrugged. It wasn't exactly like he was going to run with open arms to welcome the northern army into town—but Jackson could put a bit more effort in, darn it!

"Is Mayor Keeley in town?" Trace asked, and the sheriff nodded.

"I should think so. Unless he's up in Denver."

"Send your man." Trace nodded to Cephas. "If we're going to sort this out ourselves, then we're going to need the mayor on board as well."

Sheriff Jackson actually looked a little relieved at Trace's strong stance, and with a muttered nod, Cephas was dispatched to find Colorado City's erstwhile mayor while Annabelle gave her testimony to the sheriff.

The sheriff's station was small and barely fit for the purpose of policing a city as wild as Colorado City, but Trace saw the cabinet of guns in the back of the room and counted at least twelve long rifles. That was a good start.

"How many deputies you got now, Sheriff?" Trace asked, hovering near the window as Annabelle sat at the simple wooden desk opposite Jackson himself.

"Four. Cephas, Williams, Jody—you remember Jody? And Langton."

Trace thought he might remember half of their names. Most of them had been deputies when Trace had been young, so that put them into the white-haired and getting-ready-to-rest-their-feet-by-a-warm-fire territory.

"We'll need more. Unless you call a posse," Trace said at once. Jackson muttered something about one thing at a time and proceeded to note down Annabelle's story as she ran them through the details of the fire.

She hadn't seen who was responsible. No one had. Ever since her ranch hands had left her, she had been working every hour that God gave to keep an eye on her herd, and that meant that there were long hours when she was out on the prairie, and no eyes were on her ranch buildings.

"Ah. Well. I see." Jackson blinked.

"But *I know* it was him. The Rattler." Annabelle thumped her palm on the table. "I know what he's like. He's spiteful. Mean. He won't stop until he's got what he wants." A shudder ran down her, and Trace wanted to step forward, to put his hand on her shoulder, to show her that she was not alone—but he halted when he saw Annabelle's wary eyes flicker up at him.

Anger surged through Trace in that moment—not at Annabelle, but at what the Rattler had done to her. Annabelle was closed off, not the carefree and laughing girl he remembered. She looked at men now with distrust.

The Rattler was going to pay for this.

"The Rattler attacks ranches he wants. Or people he wants to get rid of. We know this. He planned to take our families out," Trace growled. He eyed the sheriff sternly.

"Then we send deputies to your ranches for a few days. Scare him off," Jackson pointed out.

"That's not going to cut it," Trace shook his head. "The Rattler has already waited nigh on ten years now. He's a man who knows how to be patient. A couple o' deputies for a few nights isn't going to do anything."

"And just what, Trace Cassidy, do you propose instead?" There was a cough at the door, and the portly form of Mayor Keeley, followed by Cephas, marched into the room.

Mayor Keeley was a shade of years younger than Sheriff Jackson, but not by much. His white hair still had a touch of blond to it. His waistcoat, that barely stretched over his belly, had gold buttons and green thread embroidered over black silk. He wore a dress coat as well, with wide black lapels.

And he already stank of cheap bourbon.

"Mayor." Trace turned around to regard the Mayor of Colorado City. Trace's father had always said Keeley was a low man, who was more concerned with lining his own pockets than looking after people.

Trace thought he shared that opinion.

"Colorado City has always drawn some negative attention, you know that as well as anyone, Trace." Keeley started to shake his head, as if Trace was still a teenager or a young man.

Well, I'm not anymore. Trace narrowed his eyes. He was not the boy who had gone off to war. He had seen things that he would never share with anyone.

"Ranch fires aren't negative attention, Mayor. Neither is murder in broad daylight." Trace growled. "There's been attacks on travelers to the north of the city, and the ranch burning has started up again. We're looking at a sizable group, maybe two groups if what I hear is right. And so we need to raise men. Men to keep an eye on the city, on the trails."

It all seemed pretty obvious to Trace. You needed scouts and lookouts if the enemy was nearby, didn't you? And then you also had to get intelligence on their movements...

"Men! How are we going to afford that? The city isn't rich!" Mayor Keeley said.

"The money must be going somewhere." Trace growled and eyed the mayor's gold buttons. Keeley blinked rapidly, looking surprised and shocked for a moment, but before he could say anything, Trace continued with a shrug.

"People will volunteer to protect their own," he said.

There was silence for a moment in the room, as the mayor and Annabelle glowered (each for their different reasons), and the sheriff looked thoughtful.

"That was your pa's dream, son," Sheriff Jackson said. The man nodded to Annabelle before him. "And yours. That was what they were working on, right before…"

"I know," Trace said heavily.

Before they were killed.

"I would like your support, gentlemen. But I can go it alone if I have to," Trace said firmly. The mayor bristled at that, twin spots of color rising to his cheeks, but Sheriff Jackson just sighed wearily and nodded.

"Find the men. Maybe you'd have more luck recruiting than I will, anyhow. But no one does anything rash. I can't support any vigilantes in this town." Jackson said.

If he wasn't going to do anything, then that was the only option left, Trace thought, but he still nodded all the same. "They'll report to you. They'll come back here, and you send your deputies to ride with them," he offered.

"Sounds good." Jackson nodded, reaching over to shake Trace's hand. Behind them, the mayor snorted and threw a dark glance at the pair of them before turning to walk out.

Doesn't he want to protect his city? Trace thought.

***

"We'll get advance warning now of trouble. That's something," Trace pointed out, as the pair rode back towards the ranch. Trace pictured the map of Colorado territory in his head and imagined squeezing the gangs' movements. That was the key to a successful campaign. Make it harder and harder work for them to move and operate—and hopefully they'll clear out before a shot is fired...

"That was good work today. You really know a thing or two about this, don't you?" Annabelle looked over to him.

"I picked up some in the war." Trace shrugged. He didn't want to admit that looking at maps and suggesting routes, ambushes, blocks, and escape routes had been one of his jobs. It seemed so long ago now, and like it had happened to a different person.

"So we have ten people signed up for the posse. Fifteen, if you count us as well," Annabelle said doubtfully.

"Yeah." Trace agreed with her unvoiced suspicion. After their meeting with the sheriff, Trace and Annabelle had ridden around town, talking to shop-owners and teamsters that Jackson had suggested. Everyone had been worried. Only ten had said they were willing to raise arms.

But was it enough? The riders Trace had seen murder Mr. Moat alone had numbered almost ten. And that might not have been all of the gang. And there might even be two gangs out there, as Harlan suggested.

They were going to have to be clever, Trace knew. "We have plenty of advantages. It's our terrain. We know it, we live it. And folks will be protecting their homes and families. They always fight harder than anyone."

He wondered if that was enough.

Annabelle made a sound that almost sounded like agreement, and subsided into silence for most of the rest of the journey. She surprised him when they rounded on the Cassidy ranch by suddenly turning to him and smiling—a proper smile, one of those big, knock-your-socks-off Annabelle Flint grins that Trace remembered.

"I think the mayor was scared you were going to demand he sell that darn waistcoat then and there!" she chuckled.

Trace laughed. "I should have. But how would anyone know he is the mayor without it?" Trace rolled his eyes, and Annabelle laughed.

"Oh, I am sure Keeley would find a way to tell people."

They entered the Cassidy ranch house to the smell of hot food already simmering, and the curious, puzzled faces of Frankie, Harlan, and Sawyer looking at them.

"What?" Annabelle said stubbornly, much like when her father had caught her hand-fishing in Little Creek that time and she was supposed to be milking their herd.

"We've been busy raising a posse. Shifts begin tomorrow!" Annabelle announced tartly, before marching through the kitchen to get ready for the food that was almost ready. Trace picked up one of the apples off the counter-top and munched on it as he explained the events of the day.

"Alright! Elbows up!" Frankie announced, shooing Harlan and Sawyer from the table as she heaved over a steaming iron pot to one of the small griddles. Inside, there was a whole roasted leg of ham, simmering inside a broth with garden vegetables.

"Trace—there's cornbread on the stove. Will you stop getting dust in my kitchen and bring it over?" his sister said.

"Yes, ma'am." Trace forced himself not to laugh, scuffing off his boots and his own jacket, before grabbing the iron pot with the freshly risen bread inside, and bringing it to the table. A few moments later, Annabelle reappeared, now smelling of lavender and wearing a light, white blouse and skirt. She had also let her black hair down.

"Trace! Stop staring!" Frankie hissed at him as she swished past. Trace felt a blush rise to his cheeks. He looked back at the others, but Harlan and Sawyer were already engaged in a loud argument over who deserved the most of Frankie's famous cornbread, and didn't appear to have noticed.

What was that about? What business do I have getting embarrassed around Annabelle? Trace thought, lost to his thoughts as he was surrounded by the clatter of plates.

The conversation swirled easily around them all, and it was good. Trace hadn't had an evening like this for a long time. Years, in fact. They talked about the land and about the animals, and even howled in laughter as Harlan recounted stories of just how ridiculous Mayor Keeley had been getting, year on year. No one laughed harder at Harlan's jokes than Frankie did, Trace noticed, and the reverse was also true.

Huh. He smirked to himself.

When the evening finally came to a close, Sawyer was the first to beg off, saying that he was going to ride over to the Flint ranch early tomorrow and so needed a good night's sleep. Harlan offered a pipe to Trace on the porch, and the two men wandered out to enjoy the cool night air.

The stars were out, and the sound of the women's low voices murmured behind them as Trace and Harlan shared a pinch of tobacco.

"You and my sister have gotten close," Trace said after a moment.

Instantly, Harlan blushed, then looked scared. "Well, I mean, maybe, but..."

"It's okay." Trace suppressed a chuckle. He missed Cole as much as anyone, but he also knew how good a man Cole had been. "Frankie deserves to be happy," Trace said, and it felt right.

Harlan smiled before he could stop himself. He took a puff on the pipe and handed it back over. "And what about you?"

"What about me?" Trace blinked at him in confusion.

"Annabelle. Anyone with eyes can see the air's thicker than midsummer between you two." Harlan said.

"*What?*" Trace's heart pounded. He thought of how Annabelle had looked tonight, an echo of her carefree nature returning. He could even remember how she smelled, and the way her laugh was joyous and full-throated.

Annabelle Flint had grown into a fine woman, that was for sure.

But then there was the flames. And the memory of smoke in his mind. There was his own brother's blood pumping through his hands in some East Virginian byway.

"I uh—I haven't got time for romance," Trace shook his head quickly. "It's...things are simpler that way."

Harlan opened his mouth to say something, but Trace saw him stop just as quickly. Whatever Trace's friend saw in his face, it made Harlan grimace for a moment. Harlan's hand fell firmly on Trace's shoulder in a reassuring pat.

"*You* deserve to be happy too, Trace," Harlan muttered, before he disappeared back into the kitchen. *Do I?*

Chapter Eleven

Cassidy Ranch, 1866

"You're MINE, girly. I knew it from the first time I saw ya—and I bet you did too, didn't you?"

"No!"

Annabelle gasped, turning over in her bed with the echoes of a bad dream in her ears. It had been the Rattler again, just as it had been the Rattler every night recently. Her dreams were always variations of the fire, and of the attack that killed her parents. But in each successive one, the Rattler was getting closer and closer, and in last night's dream, he had almost touched her.

It was early. The skies past the curtains were still a pre-dawn gray.

There was the slightest crunch, and a shadow moved across her window. For a moment, Annabelle was sure that she had just seen a hunched, human form.

What?

Annabelle sat bolt upright in bed, her heart hammering as she stared at the window. She couldn't hear anything, but then again, the window was closed. The spare bedroom was on the ground floor of the Cassidy ranch, and it looked out of the back of the building, towards the gardens and small barns.

Was someone out there? Had she heard the crunch of a footfall?

Annabelle wanted to believe it was just a part of the nightmare, but she couldn't let it go. She slipped out of her bed, her bare feet finding the cold floorboards as she fumbled on her bedside table for her pistol.

What if the Rattler has come for *me* here?

Her heart was in her throat as she padded through the house to the back door, easing it open just a crack as the cold night air hit her body. She avoided the creaking boards of the porch and instead hopped onto the dirt beyond and headed back towards her window.

The Rattler had told her that he wanted her. No—that he *owned* her. Annabelle felt sick at the memory and at the thought. It had nothing to do with her looks or any skill or talent she might possess. Annabelle knew that for men like the Rattler, it was only about power.

The day was still a hesitant gray, unsure whether it wanted to break into full dawn yet, and somewhere she heard a mournful cry of some bird, out on the prairie. Annabelle could hear her heart in her chest, and every crunch of her feet against the grass as she reached the end of the house, turning around.

"Annabelle?" There was a startled cough as she saw Trace stepping out of the stables, his gun already in hand. He had his overalls on and had clearly gotten up early to see to the animals in the cool of the dawn.

"Was that you? Or did you see him?" Annabelle said at once.

"See what? I was working and heard you at the back of the house." Trace frowned at her.

He gets up early to keep an eye on us all, Annabelle suddenly realized, and she told him about her dream and the shadow she saw at her window.

101

"Okay." Trace's face went deadly still. His jaw clenched. "Go back in the house. Wait for me," he said, before he moved off towards her window and the yard beyond it.

"Wait—" Annabelle started to say, but he was already gone. She remembered that she had left the kitchen door ajar, and immediately thought of Frankie inside the house, unprotected. Moving quickly, she padded back to find the door just as she had left it, and slipped inside, waiting by the kitchen table.

She waited for what felt like a long time before she heard feed padding back towards the door, and a low whistle—just like Trace used to do, back when they were kids.

"Did you find anything?" she asked in a rush as soon as she eased the door open—and stopped.

Trace had a dark look on his face, as if he had seen a ghost. Annabelle looked down at the object he held in his hands. A glove. A finely tooled, red leather glove.

"What is that?" Frankie yawned from the stairs as she walked in, dragging her shawl around her. She blinked when she saw Annabelle, still in her nightdress. "Annabelle, you'll catch your death with the door open like that."

But then Frankie's eyes boggled as she saw her brother and the object he was holding. Annabelle saw all color drain from her friend's face in an instant, and a low breath escaped her lips.

"What is it? I don't understand," Annabelle said.

"I found this outside your window," Trace said heavily. He shared a glance with his sister. "It belongs to the Rattler, I'm certain of it. It's a message."

"You get to the sheriff's," Frankie said at once. "I'll call Harlan and Sawyer in here with me. But you need to take that to the sheriff, *now*."

Annabelle had never seen Frankie so firm and self-possessed. Even when she was left running the ranch. Annabelle could see how similar Frankie and her brother were; both were as stubborn and strong as a bull when they wanted to be.

"Frankie—" Trace began, but his sister shook her head adamantly.

"The sheriff's. This is what he does. And it's about more than just us; it's about the whole community, Trace," Frankie said at once.

Annabelle saw her brother take Frankie's words on, and nodded before his strong face turned back to her own.

"You're going to be safe, Annabelle. I'm going to make sure of it." He growled the words, and Annabelle felt a quiver in her stomach. She felt something like yearning.

***

"That's just a darn glove! You can't expect me to scare the entire town over a glove and some memory you had over ten years ago!" Mayor Keeley almost shouted inside the sheriff's office.

"I know what I saw!" Trace said, and slapped the red leather glove on the sheriff's table angrily. His head was ringing. It wasn't just Mayor Keeley talking, but also Mrs. Moat—who Trace had called over—Gilligan, the theater and show-house owner, and half a dozen others of the great and good of Colorado City. Widow Moat was demanding that the mayor and the sheriff do something, while Gilligan was demanding that he not scare his clientele away, and the room seemed pretty split along those lines.

Trace's head was splitting, and he was certain that he was going to scream any moment.

"Stop this!" Sheriff Jackson said, his voice not loud but forceful. He clamped one hand down over Trace's thrown red glove, with enough of a thump that everyone in the room paused for a moment. The sheriff was not known for his displays of anger, so, on the rare times they happened, they caused double the surprise.

"Now, Keeley, we know that something is happening. We all know what happened to Mr. Moat only a few days ago," the sheriff said.

"Which might just be a bunch of drunks! Or ex-soldiers!" the mayor burst out.

Trace saw the Widow Moat bristle in outrage. She remembered the bad old days when the Rattler terrorized the ranches around here. She drew a breath, but Trace knew he had to break in before all hell broke loose.

"*I know this is scary, people!*" Trace raised his voice to say. He pointed at Gilligan. "You might lose business. You probably *are* going to lose business—just like the bakers and the feed merchants are losing business right now, because their wagons are diverting back up to Denver."

Trace nodded to Mrs. Moat. "And ma'am, you deserved to have a life with your husband. You deserved to be protected."

Finally, he turned to the sheriff. "I know you haven't got the manpower to deal with this, but that is why we rounded up some names of men willing to put the work in. We have to remember that this gang, or gangs—however many they are—

will have smaller numbers than we have. All we need is people willing to stand up. And not to give in to fear," Trace said firmly.

"Hear, hear!" Mrs. Moat clapped loudly at that, while Gilligan, the show-house owner, remained silent. Mayor Keeley rolled his eyes.

"We're not soldiers here, Cassidy. Maybe that's what your life has been like for the past few years, but out here—"

Trace saw red. His headache reached a fever pitch, and before he knew it, he was striding a few paces forward and pointing at the mayor.

"You have no idea what my life has been like, sir." Trace almost trembled with rage. "And yes, I was a soldier. And yes, that means I know how to kill people. It also means I know how to keep people safe. And that is what this city needs right now, Mayor."

Keeley's second chin quivered; he was flustered and threatened. "Well, well, hopefully it won't come to that," he said.

The meeting concluded more with a fizz than a bang, as Trace saw that some of them wanted action, but most of them—the sheriff and the mayor included—were scared.

"They don't want a war," Trace admitted to Annabelle on the ride back. In truth, he wasn't quite sure what their trip to Colorado City had done. Perhaps he shouldn't have bothered? Perhaps he should concentrate on hunting the Rattler on his own, as he had originally intended to do.

"No one wants a war, Trace. But that's the thing about wars, isn't it? Normal folks don't get to vote on them." Annabelle said heavily. "And we just have to be as ready as we can be when they come, right?"

"Yeah," Trace figured. He scratched the back of his head, feeling angry, frustrated, and confused. He knew he was ready. He knew that he had skills that were going to be useful—but Annabelle and Frankie were right. They needed to do this together if they were going to avoid a lot of bloodshed.

But Trace was sure about one thing. The Rattler wasn't going to get away this time. Not again.

"He took everything," Trace breathed. He didn't know why he said it. Maybe to try and reassure Annabelle that he knew what it was like. Maybe just because there was something about being back on his home prairie, and riding with an old friend.

"I know," Annabelle breathed, her voice soft.

"Of course you do," Trace said at once, feeling stupid. She had lost her parents to the Rattler, just like he had.

"I didn't think I could live with what you went through," Annabelle surprised him by saying.

"Me?" Trace was surprised.

"You and Frankie. But especially you. You were the oldest. It was all on you when the Rattler..." her voice trailed off.

"When he took my parents," Trace supplied. He could say it clearer now, but his voice still hitched every time. "He took *our* parents," he added, and looked over to see Annabelle looking at him, her eyes wide. "You know, I've been thinking I'm not half as strong as you are," Trace admitted, earning a sad shake of Annabelle's head.

"I didn't fight in a war," Annabelle pointed out.

"And more fool me that I did! I should have been here, looking after everyone." Trace was adamant.

106

CALICO PASS SLAUGHTER

Looking after Frankie. And you.

Annabelle was looking at him curiously, a measured, considering look on her face. "I think... you've always been a good man, Trace Cassidy. Don't let yourself ever forget that. You've always been good, and brave, and done what's right."

Trace wondered why she said that. He certainly didn't feel like a good man. Maybe if he had been a good man, Cole and Annabelle's parents would still be alive.

Maybe Wade and his parents would be too.

Chapter Twelve

Colorado City, 1866

"Skip Harrington, Buddy Miles, the Jepson family..." Annabelle creased her brow as she tried to remember the names of the people they wanted to speak to today.

She looked pretty when she was thinking, Trace couldn't help but notice.

The pair rode back to Colorado City the next day, determined to form a posse big enough to deter the Rattler.

"We can do this," Trace repeated firmly. All they needed were the numbers. And if people like Gilligan and the mayor weren't going to help—then they had better just stay out of their way.

Colorado City, like most plains cities, had wide-open access on most sides. That meant that they would see any gangs coming from a ways off, but it also meant that the gang could approach from any direction.

Apart from Pikes Peak, Trace considered. A high rise of brown and green hills, scattered with pines and maples, sat on the city's western edge. That could either give them the protection they needed—unless the gang used the narrow fox trails and windy creeks in the hills.

He kept his eyes peeled as they entered the city, the wooden buildings looming over wide streets on either side. Trace tried to determine which one any gang would most likely choose.

"Get out of it!"

A shout cut through the general city clamor, coming from the next street over. Trace glanced at Annabelle at once. It could be anything. Colorado City was full of brawlers, but...

"Let's go." Trace said, spurring Bella into a fast trot, as Annabelle did the same behind him. He made sure to put his horse ahead a little, with his hand moving to his gun as he turned the street corner.

There was a group of rough-looking teamsters surrounding Haversham Tailors, with the thin form of Mr. Haversham himself standing in front of his business and shaking his fist at them. Haversham was a walking advertisement for his shop, wearing a full tweed great coat with embroidered lapels, high-waisted trousers, and an immaculately trimmed and oiled black beard. The rough fellows around him wore hard-riding chaps over their trousers, kerchiefs, and ten-gallon hats. The contrast couldn't be any more stark.

"What's going on?" Annabelle whispered.

Trace couldn't tell. It could be drunkards wanting to start a ruckus, or an argument over an unpaid bill, or...

"*Ugh!*" The first fist landed on the exquisitely dressed Haversham and sent the man flying.

"Hey!" Trace yelled, pushing Bella forward, but not in time for the other fist to connect with the tailor, and then the boot. There was a crunch of glass as Haversham hit his own window and crumpled to the floor.

"I said, *hey!*" Trace fired his pistol in the air with a sudden crack and pushed Bella into a rearing stamp, right in front of the crowd. At once, the gang sprang backwards, drawing their guns.

"Trace!" Annabelle hissed in alarm. She was a little behind him, trying to control Prince with one hand as she had drawn her own pistol with the other.

But all at once, there was an entire gang of about eight men spread across the roadway in front of them, and all of them had guns.

"Leave him be," Trace snarled, pointing his gun straight at the largest man who had landed the first punch. The teamster was taller and more athletic than the others, with a sun-reddened skin that almost looked like leather. From the way this man smirked, Trace guessed he was the leader.

"Just a friendly conversation." The man smiled slowly and even made a show of putting his pistol back into his holster.

"Doesn't look that friendly," Annabelle said tartly.

The man directly in front of Trace looked over at Annabelle, and his smile widened just a little. Trace didn't like that one bit.

"You lot get out of here. Or you could wait for the sheriff to arrive. Your choice," Trace pointed out.

"Sheriff Jackson?" The man rolled his eyes, and several of his fellows started to chuckle. It was clear what they thought of the lawmen of Colorado City.

"Tell you what, we're on our way—but it's nice to see you again, Trace," the man pointed out.

What? Trace's frown deepened. "How do you know my name?"

But the man was still smirking, gesturing for the rest of the gang to move over to their horses, tied to the railings. They mounted with confidence, knowing that there were far more of them than Trace and Annabelle.

"I said, *how do you know my name?*" Trace demanded, pushing Bella forward. Annabelle let out a warning gasp behind him, and the ringleader wheeled around on his dark brown steed.

"The Rattler says hi, Trace. And he says you oughtta get your affairs in order. Mr. Moat wasn't us, but since you've riled the city up against my boss, well—he's mighty hurt by that. So expect trouble. The Rattler is back!"

At that, the ringleader—who was clearly some kind of lieutenant for the Rattler's gang—reared his horse into a flash of hooves, forcing Trace back. The other riders whooped, kicking their horses into stamping their hooves as they wheeled around, raising dust before they broke into a gallop up the road, and out of town.

"Mr. Haversham!" Annabelle was the first to run to the tailor, who was bleeding from his nose and lip, but appeared more shaken than anything else.

Trace quietened Bella as the Rattler's gang turned from a thunder into a distant growl of dust on the horizon. There were shouts from the other end of the street as fellow shopkeepers emerged out of their establishments once the danger had gone, and ran forward to check everyone was okay.

"Someone ride to get Sheriff Jackson," Trace said. He felt like he had been slapped. His entire body trembled with anger.

It was happening. It was him. The Rattler was indeed back.

Chapter Thirteen

Cassidy Ranch, 1866

"That's the last one fitted." Sawyer groaned as he straightened up from the window and rattled the heavy-duty wooden shutter, with the crossbeam on the inside holding it closed.

"Nice work." Trace looked up from where he was collecting the woodworking tools and sweeping the shavings from the floor. They were in the main ranch house, and from somewhere, he could hear the muted sounds of laughter as Frankie and Harlan were clearly more engrossed with each other than they were with securing the family home.

"Ah, you can't fault them." Sawyer saw the dour look on Trace's face and broke into a grin. "What's all this for, if people can't have fun, huh?"

"Yeah, I guess so," Trace said. He didn't mind his sister having fun. And he knew Harlan—Sawyer's son—to be a good man. One of the best, in fact.

But sometimes he wished that others saw the danger as clearly as he did. Sometimes he got the notion that the war had put something into him that he could never get rid of. He felt like there was a part of him that he had almost managed to put to sleep—but now it was back.

"And what about you and Annabelle? I thought I saw something between you there the other night..?" Sawyer said evenly as they stood up. The new shutters were in place in the windows, and even though Trace had no faith that they would hold against a determined attack—the Rattler's gang could just use axes or even set fire to the ranch, after all—they would buy them some time.

Trace remained stoically silent as they walked out of the house, heading for the barn where he intended to put a new heavy-duty lock on the door. Again, he wasn't sure if it would do anything other than give them precious few minutes if they were attacked...but it might stop anyone from skulking around.

Trace waited until he was sure that Frankie and Harlan were out of earshot before shrugging at Sawyer.

"We've always been close," Trace admitted, and it was truer than he wanted to admit. He got a warm feeling when he thought about Annabelle, her bravery, her sudden laughter—and her looks.

"Yeah, but close as chillun and close as adults are two different things," Sawyer teased lightly.

Yes. They were. Trace paused in front of the barn. That was the problem, wasn't it? He didn't know if Annabelle even liked him, not really. If they hadn't grown up together, and if their families hadn't been so close—would she even look at him twice?

"I uh, I need to focus on the Rattler right now." Trace said hurriedly, feeling vaguely clumsy and slow-witted for some reason.

What could a woman like Annabelle Flint see in a killer like him, anyway?

"Who's that?" Sawyer hissed, and Trace turned at once to see the old man pointing down their track to where a small cloud of dust was approaching. It grew steadily larger and larger, resolving into two riders, who appeared to be riding hell for leather towards them.

"Rifles," Trace said at once, running back towards the house to grab two of the long Sharps rifles he kept beside the front door, and checking to see if they were loaded.

The two riders kept coming. They didn't slow down one bit. Frankie and Harlan emerged from the house looking concerned, and Trace waved them back in hurriedly, before walking out—alone—into the middle of the yard.

"If they're going to come for anyone, then they'll have to go through me," Trace growled, and raised his rifle.

"Don't shoot! Don't shoot!"

Trace recognized that voice. A moment later, he saw the flash of silver hair under the hat. It was Sheriff Jackson and his deputy, Cephas.

"Jackson!" Trace said in alarm, dropping his rifle at once as the two riders started to slow their thunder, turning a gallop into a canter as they reached the Cassidys' main yard.

"Cassidy, you gotta come to town," Jackson panted. His face looked drawn and tight with worry. Trace didn't think he had ever seen the man so energized.

"Mayor Keeley has been shot. Right outside the playhouse. He's at the infirmary right now—but there's more," the sheriff said gravely, and flashed a look to Sawyer at his side, as Frankie and Harlan watched from the open door. It was clear there was something he needed to say, but couldn't in front of the others.

"Okay. Wait a minute while I saddle up. Do you want water? Lemonade?" Trace asked, as Sawyer went to grab a pitcher, and Trace ran to the stables. By the time he came out, he could see that the sheriff was eager to get going, draining the glass of lemonade and wheeling his horse around.

"Let's go," Trace said.

***

"I've had some suspicions for a long time now," Sheriff Jackson admitted as they trotted into town, muttering the words so only Trace would hear.

"About Mayor Keeley?" Trace asked. His eyes scanned the streets to see that they were curiously quiet today. Some of the shops, although they had their doors open, had left the shutters on their windows, and several hadn't even opened at all.

Colorado City was scared. Even the bordellos and saloons seemed subdued after the attacks.

"He's strangled the funds coming to my office every year. And every time I push for more guns or more recruits, he argues against it. I asked him for funds to patrol the hills. He flat-out denied it and wouldn't investigate all the claims that have been handed over through the years. And, well, we all know that he's been getting richer year upon year."

"Hmm," Trace agreed soberly. It would be a bad business if the sheriff was proved right. There were plenty of ranchers who had sold their claims at rock-bottom prices, or had merely upped and left after a barn got torched.

"You know, when I was hunting the Rattler, I went through Pa's things," Trace said seriously. "He thought the Rattler was buying up gold claims wherever he could, or just threatening the families who sat on land claims, making them give *him* the land."

Trace paused as they rounded on the low, long white building that was the Colorado City Infirmary.

"And land claims mean a paper trail," the sheriff said.

"A paper trail that someone had to clean up," Trace finished. It wasn't proof that the sheriff had been involved with the Rattler—but someone official enough had to have been. Trace knew his pa had never managed to get to the bottom of it before he died, and every rock that Trace had overturned had revealed nothing but dust.

They tied their horses and entered the pristine building, which smelled strongly of soap and acrid rubbing alcohol. A small waiting area held a few Colorado City patrons (mostly drunkards with a bump or two on their heads), but they led the way through the open archway and into the much wider hall beyond.

Beds were set up throughout the hall, with curtains pulled to screen off a few of them. Trace heard a few moans and heard a few low, pained coughs.

"Sheriff?" It was the ancient Doctor Kilgore, emerging from behind one of the screens with his stethoscope in his hands. The principal doctor of Colorado City was hunched over and peering through thick bottle glasses.

"How is he?" Jackson said, with a touch of baritone steel to his voice. Trace was starting to be impressed by Sheriff Jackson. Maybe he had misjudged him—or maybe the sheriff was finally waking up.

"He's stable, and as long as he doesn't get an infection, then I would say the prognosis is good. But he needs to rest," Kilgore attempted to say, as the sheriff marched past him, and Trace followed.

"Aberneezer Keeley," the sheriff announced as he stepped past the curtain. Trace made sure to pull the curtain closed behind them, despite Doctor Kilgore looking bothered on the other side.

The Mayor of Colorado City lay on one of the narrow beds, his form mounded in a swathe of white blankets. Trace couldn't see any visible wounds on his face and upper arms, but his eyes were surrounded by deep shadows, and his skin had a sickly yellowish hue.

"Sheriff? Trace!" Keeley looked surprised to see them both, but then a look of fear creased his brow. Trace could tell that the man knew what this was going to be about.

"I–I already told you what happened, Jackson." Keeley tried to rally himself, but as soon as he attempted to push himself up the bed, he hissed in pain, one hand moving to the spot on the blankets where his belly was covered.

"You did. But I wanted you to repeat it for Trace, here, seeing as he's our man taking point on this," Jackson said, pulling the only chair in the small, curtained-off cubicle and sitting down on it with a groan. The sheriff didn't seem mad anymore, just tired.

"You were shot by someone right here in town. And eye witnesses say it wasn't just one someone, but a whole gang of men who came for you," the sheriff prodded.

"Yes, well... Colorado City has an unfortunate history of violence..." Keeley started to mutter—but Trace could see he was already a broken man. Injury had hollowed him out and stripped him of his anger.

"And someone said they overheard one of the men shouting at you, Keeley.", Jackson went on to say. If anything, the sheriff sounded even more tired than before.

Not tired—disappointed.

"They did?" A look of fright crossed Aberneezer Keeley's face.

The sheriff nodded slowly. "Tell us, Mayor. Just tell us why the man who shot you was shouting 'this is what you get when you side with the Rattler!'"

"What?" Trace couldn't stop his angry hiss. He clutched the rails at the end of the bed until his knuckles turned white.

Could it be true? Could the *m*ayor really be on the Rattler's payroll? The man had killed his parents!

Keeley threw a worried glance at Trace, and back at the sheriff. "I...I never meant it to go like this. I promise. I knew nothing about any of his attacks, I swear!"

"*Tell us, Keeley,*" Trace demanded, his voice a low snarl. He wanted to drag him out of his bed right here and now, but he wouldn't do that to an injured man.

The mayor's lip wobbled for a moment before he broke down in a rush. "You were right, Trace. There are two gangs out there. It wasn't the Rattler who shot me, it was the other one."

"Because you are working for the man who killed not only my parents, but almost all the Flint family as well?" Trace couldn't stop himself.

"It didn't start like that, I promise!" Keeley said. "The Rattler was another prospector, like everyone else. He lost his own family to a ranch attack and came here... and he threatened my daughter. He said if I didn't help him with the claims, then I would never see her again. He told me he would make sure of it!"

The mayor broke down into tears, and Trace once again resisted the urge not to shout at him. He was a weak man, that was all. He had not an ounce of grit in him.

"You should have come to us." Trace glared at the mayor. "You were elected to help protect the people of Colorado City, and if you had come to us—your neighbors, your business partners—then we would have protected you."

"I know. I know I should have. But I was so scared... and now that the new gang is here, what can I do? If I don't get killed by one, then the Rattler will take my Sarah-Jane!" Keeley sniffed.

"Sheriff?" Trace muttered, for Jackson to nod.

"I'll see to it. She can stay at mine for now."

"*What is going on in there?*" The irate voice of Doctor Kilgore was followed by the very irate form of the doctor just a few moments later, as he stuck his head through the gap in the curtain and looked shocked at the state the mayor was in.

"Really, this will not do. The man's humors need to be calm—*calm!*" the doctor yelled in a less-than-calm way. Before Kilgore could tell them to get out, the mayor sniffed and spoke up.

"But—there's something else. It's Annabelle. It's about Annabelle Flint," Keeley said.

"What do you mean?" Trace said at once, taking a step around the side of the bed towards him.

"The Rattler wants her now, and only her. It started out as land claims, but he's got obsessed. The other gang are pressing him, and he's become rabid." The mayor looked up at Trace.

"He only cares about having Annabelle Flint now."

Trace felt ice-cold run down his spine. Just like the red glove outside the window. It was a message. And the gang, too, the other day in town.

119

ZACHARY MCCRAE

"That's not going to happen." Trace growled. He nodded at the sheriff, and both men got up to leave.

"Annabelle Flint? The Rattler? What is going on here?" They heard Doctor Kilgore's confused voice behind them—but they kept on walking.

Chapter Fourteen

Cassidy Ranch, 1866

"Careful now, he can get a bit flighty."

Annabelle listened to Trace fretting over one of their young stallions, a black horse named Champion, and wondered if Trace knew her at all.

"I think I know my way around an ornery horse, Trace," she scoffed.

They were in the Cassidy stables, and Trace had been adamant that he help Annabelle out with the feed.

What is up with him lately?

Annabelle watched Trace surreptitiously as they worked. Ever since he had come back from the city a few days ago, he had been running around like he was being chased by a cloud of bees. He was more closed off than even his usual dour self, and it was beginning to feel like every time she turned around, he was there.

But then again, he had changed after coming back from the war, hadn't he? A flash of sadness clutched at her heart. The Trace Cassidy she remembered from before all this had been leggy, and wild, and bold. He had been their natural, daring leader, always pushing them to explore the creeks and hills much farther than their parents would ever want them to.

The young Trace had also been quick to laugh, and even quicker to jump and shout.

And all of that was taken from him by the war—and the Rattler...

"Of course you do, Annabelle. My apologies, I just know he can be ten types of difficult if he wants to be." Trace cast a quick look at the door. He appeared distracted, like he was always waiting for something.

"Okay, Trace. Let's hear it." Annabelle threw the last fork of fresh hay in Champion's stall and leaned against the handle, eyeing him.

"Hear what?" Trace said off-handedly. He frowned as he looked at the open stable door.

"Trace!" Annabelle said—before there was the sudden jangle of harnesses, and a shout from their yard.

"Stay back!" Trace's voice was tight. He dropped the feed bag he had been holding and sprang for the door, his hand going to the fun at his hip that he hadn't taken off for the last few days.

"Whoa there!"

Annabelle heard Frankie's laugh, shocked and excited at the same time, and heard a low murmur of voices. She sighed, setting the feed bag out of Champion's reach before marching out, brushing off the flying strands of hay and stray from her overalls.

Frankie and Harlan were dismounting from their own horses, and beaming as only a young couple in love can beam.

Uh-oh. Annabelle could guess at once what was going on. No one looks that happy unless...

"We're going to get married!" Frankie burst out, breaking from Harlan's side to run—not to Trace, but to Annabelle.

"Oh!"

It was hard for Annabelle not to feel some of her friend's joy, and she grinned, hugging her back. It's not like Annabelle hadn't seen this coming a mile off.

"Oh, Frankie. I'm so pleased for you," Annabelle whispered into Frankie's ear.

In front of them, the two men were taking things a whole lot more seriously. Harlan held out his hand for Trace to grip.

"Trace, I know that, well... there isn't a Mr. Cassidy to ask now, so I thought that I would ask you directly. I intend to take your sister's hand in marriage, and I need to know if you are going to be okay with that," Harlan said steadily.

For a moment, Trace stiffened, and Annabelle seriously thought he was going to refuse. But then he clasped the slightly younger man's hand, and Frankie squealed in delight.

"Of course, you have my blessing. I can see that you make Frankie very happy. I just..." Trace winced. "Is *now* the right time? Really... *now?* With the Rattler out there..." Trace looked concerned, and Annabelle had a terrible premonition that he was going to ruin all of it.

"Trace! Actually, I think now is the perfect time for it!" Frankie called out. "If there's anything that our life has taught us, then it is we have to be happy. We have to seize life right now, don't we?"

Trace frowned at that, but nodded all the same.

Wasn't that exactly what he had hoped he was doing when he returned home after the war? Annabelle thought. She saw him shake Harlan's hand a little firmer.

He still isn't happy, Annabelle thought. But she could see the same faraway look on his face as he scanned the horizon, constantly looking for threats.

"I think you're doing the right thing." Annabelle turned to Frankie. "Now, go kiss your fiancé before Trace crushes his hand."

***

"No, I'm supportive, I really am—I just think it's all a bit...rushed," Trace muttered as Annabelle found him in the main house, trying his best to tie his kerchief into something like a cravat.

"They're almost ready. Come here." Annabelle sighed heavily, marching up to him to unlace the silk kerchief and instead folding it under the collar of his shirt. With a few twists, she managed to turn it into a bow.

Trace Cassidy wore his war uniform, and from the smell of the polish in the air, she could tell that he had spent hours polishing the buttons and the boots until they shone. He had even managed to find a few pins to put in his lapel, and in his hand, he clutched a roll of cloth awkwardly.

"What's that?" Annabelle asked.

Trace looked awkward and uncomfortable. He opened his hand to reveal a white handkerchief, and inside it was a small silver hair pin, with a blue stone.

"It was our Mam's. I figured that if I'm going to walk her down the aisle—or across the lower paddock, at least—then she should wear this." His voice was thick with emotion as he looked down at what was probably the last remnant of their parents.

"Oh, Trace. That's beautiful," Annabelle said, putting her hand gently on Trace's arm. The air thickened between them, and she was suddenly aware of how close he was, of the tang of wood smoke and healthy animal scent of him.

"*Anna!* We're out of time!" Frankie's voice cut through the moment, and both Annabelle and Trace jumped back as if stung. Annabelle felt a blush blossom in her cheeks, and she hid it by turning.

"Frankie's desperate. We need to go," Annabelle said, turning and purposefully *not* noticing the way that Trace's cheeks had blushed a deep red for a moment.

They hurried back down the stairs to the main hall, where Annabelle was standing with one hand on her hip and a bouquet of flowers—and she looked dazzling. She had the same waves of chestnut-gold hair that Trace did, but on her they were long and ran down just past the nape of her neck, and she had brushed it until it gleamed.

She wore a blue dress, made of a light material but with a white corset that showed off her hips and curves. A spray of meadow flowers that Annabelle had picked this morning rounded her head.

"I know none of it costs a lot, but..." Frankie said awkwardly.

"You look beautiful," Annabelle smiled, and stepped back as Trace congratulated her and gave her the hair pin. She burst out into tears, and then hit him for making her cry, and then hugged him.

"Right. Enough of that. Any more crying and I'll call the whole thing off. So let's get this done!" Frankie said, as Trace took her arm and they stepped out of the front door, with Annabelle following close behind.

125

They stepped out into the brilliant sun, to a smatter of applause and sighs from the assembled. It was only the very next day after Harlan and Frankie's announcement, and Annabelle knew that no one had much time to prepare—but she saw the Wurts from the other side of the creek had made it, as had the Evans. Even Widow Moat had managed to ride up this morning. Really, all Frankie had wanted was her close family nearby, but people had shown up.

And we're all family, in a way.

The priest, Father Hoffler, stood at the gate entrance to the paddock, ready to escort them to the small arbor of flowers that Trace and Annabelle had had a devil of a time putting up this morning. Annabelle saw grins on everyone's faces, and Sawyer and Harlan were standing by the priest; Harlan was wearing his finest jacket and high trousers, and smiling as though he was the luckiest man alive...which Annabelle thought was only proper.

"Alright, everyone—let's get this over and done with!" Frankie shouted and stepped off the porch...

...just as gunshots split the air.

***

"Frankie—back in the house!" Trace yelled, as Annabelle spun to see that there was a group of riders on the edge of the hard, with rifles pointed at their guests.

Another shot split the air, and on the other side of the yard, another three men jumped from between the barns, lowering rifles at the crowd.

"Nobody move!" One of the men yelled, and Annabelle saw that it was the same one who had threatened Trace after beating up Mr. Haversham. It was the tall, athletic one with blond hair.

Trace had thrown himself forward in front of Frankie and Annabelle, his hands spread out in front of them both. Annabelle grabbed Frankie by the arm and pulled her back towards her, covering her with her own arms.

"No one needs to get hurt!" the leader said, swaggering forward and gesturing with his rifle. "Come on now, on the ground. You all know how this works. I want to see everyone on their asses before I force them, and your hands in the air!"

"Trace!" Frankie hissed in Annabelle's arms, and she could see Trace's look of frustration. There were only seven of the gang here, but they were in two groups, and at any moment, they could open fire either on the guests—or them.

He's come for me, hasn't he? Annabelle thought, scanning the bandits but not seeing the one face that she was looking for.

He wasn't here. The Rattler wasn't here. What did that mean?

Annabelle knew that she should be scared. She knew that she should be terrified, even—but somehow she felt nothing. All that she felt was a terrible, cold certainty. She knew what she needed to do. Maybe she had known for days, really, but hadn't admitted it to herself.

"I'm only here to deliver a message, on behalf of the Rattler— you hear me?" the man sneered at them, dropping his rifle as the rest of the gang swept back and forth over the assembled guests.

The lieutenant walked forward to where the long trestle table had been set out by the paddock fence, with a selection of sandwiches under covers, fresh fruit, and the pan breads and pound cakes that people had brought.

Everyone watched as he peeked under one of the white doilies, looked impressed, and reached in to grab a handful of the pound cake, drizzled with maple syrup, straight from the tin. Crumbs ran down his shirt and spilled from his dirty gloves.

"Mighty shame you never invited us, I have to say. Not very *neighborly* of you." The blond-haired bandit laughed.

Frankie let out a low, furious moan, and Annabelle saw Harlan rise to his feet.

"*Don't!*" she shouted, and as quick as a flash, the lieutenant outlaw had drawn his pistol and leveled it against Harlan.

"Don't hurt him!" Trace demanded, slowly rising from his crouch, his hands up.

"Aww, simmer down, soldier boy." The man laughed, wiping his hand on the table cloth as he turned to Trace. "Like I say, we didn't come here looking for trouble. What we *did* come here for is to give you a little message. The Rattler sends his greetings, and he wants you to give over your town to him."

"Colorado City?" Sawyer, standing beside his son Harlan, burst out in disbelief.

"You heard me, old-timer!" The outlaw turned back as quick as a flash. "You are going to give the Rattler Colorado City, lock, stock, and barrel, or you will feel his wrath. It's very simple. And he has a message for someone very particular in this audience, too."

Annabelle waited for the inevitable, and of course, the bandit's eyes picked *her* out of all the people here.

"Annabelle Flint, the Rattler has a special message just for you", the outlaw announced, gesturing with his pistol at her. "The Rattler sends his greetings and says that he knows that

128

the two of you will be together. He hasn't forgotten you, and you will be his."

Cold ran through Annabelle, as every sinew of her body wanted to scream—no—and yet, somehow she couldn't bring the word out of her mouth. She felt like she was a caged bird, caught in a trap and with no way out.

"You've said your piece—now get out of here!" Trace bellowed. He looked beside himself with rage, as if he didn't care that there were guns pointing at him.

Annabelle felt in a daze. Maybe this was all inevitable. Maybe there really was nothing that she could have done about any of this...

"This is *my* sister's wedding, and I'm telling you to clear off. *Now!"* Trace roared, standing straight and shaking a fist in the air. The assembled crowd gasped in fear and concern—but the outlaw captain just laughed, raising his pistol to tip his hat at Trace before sauntering away, and back to his men.

They clearly weren't afraid of an unarmed Trace. Or of anything.

Chapter Fifteen

Western Colorado Territories, 1866

So soon!

The future was so close that Axel could almost taste it, as he looked out of the cracked window in his ranch house, at the high-wooded hills around him. The outlaw knew that, for now, his office and this entire ranch might look as though it was in a state—but in his mind, he had transformed it into what it was always meant to be.

What it *would* be, as soon as he had Annabelle Flint.

The wood paneling and the brass fixtures would gleam with polish. There would be a proper antique sideboard in the corner, and a map of *The Bishop Territory* hanging on the wall.

"The Bishop Territory? Bishop *Free* Territory. Axel *Free* Territory..."

The Rattler rolled some of the names over in his mouth to see which one of them sounded the most prestigious. In truth, it had been such a long time since he had recognized his birth name of Bishop that it felt strange to be calling his upcoming kingdom that.

And it reminded him of his father. Which was never a good thing.

Axel's hand shook so much that he had to set the glass tumbler down on the desk lest he throw it against the wall. *No.* His vile, abusive parents were dead. Killed by ranch-attackers just as he did the same to others now.

And he wanted nothing of his father's name to live on. What had that man ever given him but pain? And it was from a life of pain that Axel had carved a new path for himself as the Rattler.

Rattler.

Maybe it should just be something as simple as *Rattle-Snake County.* That sounded good, didn't it?

Axel was calmed by the dreams of his future conquest, and he was calmed by the knowledge that it would all come to pass once he had Annabelle. That was who she was—didn't anyone else see the glow of nobility around her?

She was the one who got away—but that was because he, the great Rattler, once Axel Bishop, hadn't been ready before. The man had been forced to transform a lot in his life, and now, he saw why that had been. He had turned himself from Axel Bishop into the Rattler, and from the Rattler, he would have to transform into something else.

Someone worthy of having complete control of an entire territory, of course!

This thought brought him a measure of peace, and he toasted his assured future victory—all of which relied on him winning Annabelle.

"She is the key, you see?" Axel murmured to no one but the cobwebs and himself. There was something about her. Something that would provide him with the legitimacy and the *dynasty* that his greatness required.

"Boss?" A series of sharp knocks disturbed his reverie, and Briggs, all six feet of athletic muscle and topped with blond hair, walked in.

"Report." Axel's voice was sharp, authoritarian. He knew what he needed to project in order to inspire his troops.

In return, Briggs stood a little taller, a little straighter. "They got the mayor. Clay's men shot him a couple days ago, I think to stir them up against us."

"And the message?" Axel snapped. The mayor was an annoyance, but he wasn't the key. The plan had progressed too far to worry about land claims any more.

He saw a momentary wince cross Brigg's face, and Axel wondered if he would have to discipline him for that. The younger man was good at his job, but recently he had been getting a little...argumentative. Especially around the issue of Annabelle Flint.

He wasn't a believer. And that could be a problem.

"I delivered your message personally to her, boss. They were having a wedding."

"*What?*" Axel felt his heart seize in his chest. No. That wasn't right. That wasn't what was supposed to happen. It was that soldier, wasn't it? Trace Cassidy.

"The sister." Briggs' voice was hurried. "The younger Cassidy sister was getting married. I told Annabelle what you said, and I told everyone your terms."

"Give me the town." Axel nodded with a sigh of relief. So, Annabelle wasn't the one getting married. She had some sense left. This meant that she actually knew what was best for her. She knew that she was destined to be with him, the Rattler.

"Yes, boss. But—there's still Clay Slade out there..." Briggs started to say.

"Clay Slade is still wet behind the ears. He has no idea what it takes to run a territory." Axel shook his head dismissively.

Another slight frown crossed Brigg's features, and Axel's quick eyes caught it. *Yes.* He might have to have a word with Briggs before all this was over. Perhaps Briggs wasn't the man he needed to see it through to the end.

"Our man on the inside thinks he's planning another attack on the town. He's got about eight good gunslingers, and about three saloons are paying him protection money." Briggs said slowly and carefully.

"Good." Axel grinned.

"Good?" Briggs's eyebrows shot up. "But—if Clay Slade takes the town, then it'll make our job much harder..."

"Fool." Axel snarled at him. His voice turned into a low chuckle. "Tell our man on Clay's gang to support the idea in every way he can. Get Slade to attack the town. He'll waste his bullets and hopefully will lose half his men in the fight...and when the town is reeling – *we'll* get the spoils."

"Right. You *want* Clay Slade to make a play for Colorado City. You *want* the locals to get riled up." Briggs said slowly, as if he were trying to see sense in it. "Won't that just make the locals even more committed to fighting? Up to now, there have been families leaving town, and panic is setting in. If they knuckle down..."

"They're drunkards and ranchers, Briggs!" Axel slammed his fist on the tabletop. "What do they know of war? Let them think they can take a petty, small man like Clay Slade on—and then the Rattler will show them what a *real* leader looks like!"

"Right, boss." Briggs said faintly. He looked about to say something, but then didn't.

Wise, thought Axel. Because another word of argument from his second would see him pushing up daisies in a dirt bath.

"See that it's done, Briggs, and prepare my men. You are about to witness history in the making."

"Of course—*sir.*" Briggs said, his voice small as he backed out of the room.

Yes. The time was almost upon them. Axel could feel the storm gathering in the air. Very, very soon, he would be king of Rattlesnake Free County.

And he would have Annabelle Flint by his side, as his wife.

Chapter Sixteen

Cassidy Ranch, 1866

The strong Colorado winds hit Trace as he looked up from the fence he was mending. Annabelle was striding across his yard towards the stables, with Sawyer behind her. She was dressed in trousers and with her heavy, outer green jacket on.

"Annabelle? Where are you going?" He dropped his tools without thinking, running across the yard as one hand went to his gun belt. Had something happened? Were they under attack?

"Trace, not this again." Annabelle stopped in her tracks, looking flustered as both he and Sawyer caught up with her.

"I'm going out. Sawyer has just told me that one of the older sows on my ranch is having trouble milking, and it's my job to sort it out." Annabelle sighed, moving to step around Trace.

Trace stepped quickly between her and the stables. "Annabelle, please. We agreed that you needed to stay here and stay safe."

Annabelle pulled herself up abruptly and fixed him with a hard eye. "Trace Cassidy, I am going to ask you to get out of my way, and I am going to ask you nicely. But don't make me ask twice. I can't just stay here on your ranch all the time! I feel like a prisoner!"

Frustration surged through Trace. He could see the fire sparking in Annabelle's eyes, and he knew that she was good for her word and would likely take a swing at him if he opposed her.

But he was trying to save her life.

"You feel like a prisoner?" he said softly. He had never wanted her to feel like that. That was the last thing he ever wanted her to feel.

Annabelle blinked and shrugged. "Well. I can't go anywhere I want to go, not on my own, anyway. And how long is this going to go on for? I can't spend the rest of my life here, can I?"

She was right, of course. Trace had no idea she felt this way. Or that he had been *making* her feel this way.

"I just wanted you to be safe." Trace murmured. "No—I *need* you to be safe."

Annabelle frowned a little at that and looked exasperated. "Well, I don't remember you needing to be this protective when we were younger, Trace."

"Things are different now." He spoke before thinking, the words bursting out of him. "You—you're a part of my family, Annabelle. Always have been. You've lost so much, I've lost so much—we all have." He hesitated, but knew he had to get the words out. He had to make her see how important this was to him.

"I don't think I could bear it if something happened to you, too."

In front of him, Annabelle was silent for a moment, and her eyes wouldn't meet his. Had he gone too far? Said too much? Had he made her see just how much she meant to him?

"I get that." Her voice was quiet and somber. "And I thank you for it, and for letting me stay here. But I guess...I just need to be doing something. *We* need to be doing something—fighting back. We can't sit around in our homes, waiting for the Rattler to pick us off."

She raised her head and looked him in the eyes. Her eyes were a pristine, clear green, and they were mesmerizing.

"Your sister is right, you know, when times are harsh, we need to do everything we can to continue with life, not run away from it." Annabelle said steadily. "Otherwise, what are we fighting for?"

Her words hit Trace's mind like a hammer. How long had it been since he had really *lived* his life? Had celebrated it? Enjoyed it? He guessed that was what he wanted to do after the war—but then this had happened.

The only moments he truly remembered being happy recently had been with Frankie and Sawyer and Harlan—and with Annabelle.

"Okay. But I don't want you to go alone. I'll come with you." Trace said—just as the sound of furious hooves rose on their track.

The trail that led to the Cassidy ranch was wide, but it skirted the bottom of a grassy hill. The rider had managed to get close before they could see the dust.

Aww, hell! Trace swore, turning at once towards the open gate, with his pistol jumping into his hand.

"It's Cephas!" Annabelle called out as she shielded her eyes from the sun. A moment later and Trace could see what she saw, the same larger bulk of the deputy, and the glint of the star on his breast.

Cephas was riding hard, and Trace could tell that something was up.

"I'll get the rifles," Sawyer said, breaking into a run for the house as Trace ran towards the deputy.

"Cassidy! The sheriff says come quick. One of the gangs has attacked the city, and they're taking people hostage!" Cephas called out.

Trace felt a chill run down his spine, but it wasn't fear. It was action. His head felt clear, and his movements smooth and liquid as he knew that the time was here.

He had been called to protect his folk—and that was what he was going to do.

***

"He's calling himself Clay Slade, and he's got them in Gilligan's saloon bar," Cephas said as they slowed their horses at the first sight of the city buildings.

"The saloon bar?" Trace winced. That made things difficult. Gilligan owned and ran the playhouse and theater, but right next to those, with the same connected brickwork, was the smaller Gilligan's Saloon Bar, which was an up-market establishment, mostly for visiting patrons to the playhouse itself. There was one side street on the far side of it, but it was protected on almost all sides.

"How many?" Trace asked, eyeing the first of the warehouses as they neared them. Plumes of dark smoke were rising in the north of the town, where Cephas said that Clay Slade's gang had already set fire to the mill and another warehouse, before grabbing people off the street.

"There were five when the sheriff told me to go get you. But it could be more by now." Cephas said.

"And the sheriff is at the saloon bar?" Trace pulled his horse to a stop. He couldn't see any look-outs at the sides of the buildings or under the odd tree—but that didn't mean that they weren't there.

"Yes, sir," Cephas nodded. "He has the other deputies and most of the men you recruited in the posse. They've got the street locked down, but Clay is holed up tighter than a rat in a hole in there."

"Hmm." Trace looked at Harlan beside him, whose face was somber. He was young, and he was brave—but he had never fought in any war.

And Frankie would kill me if I got her new husband shot.

"You're going to be with the sheriff's forces, Harlan. I need a man I know well there," Trace said. Harlan didn't bat an eyelid, but nodded at once.

"But for now, we're going to go in slowly. Keep an eye on the streets around you *and* the windows and rooftops. If you see movement, you duck and holler, you got that?" Trace said to the two men beside him.

There wasn't enough time to introduce them to the basics of soldiering, and certainly not enough time to turn them into trained army scouts—but Trace endeavored to at least tell them what he could.

"We leave our horses out here. We'll lose the ability to chase them, and we'll lose the speed—but horses just get in the way in a town situation," Trace admitted, and nodded to a stand of bristlecone pines where they could tether their beasts. That done, Trace had them hide away any loud colors, be it kerchiefs or undershirts, and told Cephas to take his deputy badge off.

"What? But that's my job, Cassidy!" Cephas objected, but Trace shook his head.

"It also points a great big target right on your chest. If you want to make it through today, you take it off. Your friends will recognize you anyway, and those who aren't your friends, well—that's what we have these for, right?" Trace raised his

Springfield repeater. He had his pistol on his hip at the same time, but he hoped not to use it, in truth. If he had to end up using his six shooter, then that meant the fighting had gotten up close and personal.

They neared the outer warehouses and could clearly hear the clang of the fire bell, as doubtless the fire wagon was being hauled out to the burning buildings.

"They were smart in some ways." Trace muttered. "The sheriff will have to divide his forces to fight the fire and keep the gang locked down here."

Cephas nodded. "That's why he said to get you. He said you would know what to do."

Trace nodded. He did. His eyes no longer saw Tilman's Feed Store and Colorado City Storage barns. Instead, years of experience awakened in him, as he cataloged vantage points, escape routes, and pinch points.

They were still a couple of streets away when they heard the first sound of raised shouts. It wasn't a clamor, and it sounded more like someone bragging than it did a desperate call to arms.

"Down there." He pointed down one of the side streets between the stores, that would lead them to the far end of the street where Gilman's businesses stood. The three men ran down the side street, keeping to the shadow of the buildings as Trace went first, checking the rooftops and windows. There was a bang of shutters, as those townsfolk who had stayed were hurriedly seeking to defend themselves in the best way they could.

There was a small crowd of people at the end of the street, and Trace recognized the sheriff's white hair under his hat. They were waiting at the edge of the buildings, and someone had brought out crates for them to sit beside or behind.

"A siege isn't going to work," Trace said at once, recognizing what Sheriff Jackson must be thinking.

"Trace." The older man tipped his hat. "We got more numbers than them. All we got to do is wait them out."

Trace shook his head. "You're right about the numbers, but a siege requires dedication. And meanwhile, you've got people living right opposite, and this Clay Slade guy can threaten to kill the hostages. His demands will only get worse with every hour that this continues."

Jackson was flustered, his bushy white eyebrows beetling as he sucked air through his teeth. "Well, darn it—what do you suggest? If we rush him, then we're just going to get a lot of people killed!"

"What do we know about him?" Trace asked, bending low as he moved to the front of the crates and peered around the edge of the building.

The street was wide and dominated by Gilligan's Playhouse, standing in the center. Trace saw the upper-story windows of the round building and the smaller saloon built onto the side of it. Two men with rifles stood outside the saloon door—and they were mean-looking. One had curly black hair, while the other chewed on a stick, glaring up and down the street in front of him.

The sheriff shifted in his crouch. "We received a telegram at the Denver sheriff's office this morning. They say they've known about Clay Slade for a while. Apparently, he was a Union soldier, but deserted during the war. The Denver sheriff *already* suspected him of robbing a postal wagon before the war, and since then, his name has been tied to a whole lot of attacks on travelers in the Denver area."

"I get the picture." Trace nodded. He had met people like that during the war. People who should never been a soldier. People who were bad before they ever put on a uniform.

Of course, there were those soldiers that did their duty as best they could—some for the flag they believed in, or the state they came from, and some like Trace, for the family and friends they had around them.

But then, there were others who dropped out, ran off, or deserted real quick when they saw how hard it was. Usually, those men were escaping something in their old lives and saw the service as a chance to start again. But then there were those who signed up because they liked the feel of a six-iron in their hands, and they liked the fear they saw in the eyes of their victims. *These* were the sort of men that Clay Slade belonged to. It was no surprise he picked on weaker targets like travelers.

"Then this must be his first big break," Trace reasoned, watching the men outside the saloon. They looked mean enough. But anyone could point a gun and shoot.

"It sure is a long way from attacking caravans to trying to take over an entire town," Jackson muttered, crouching down with the creak of aging bones beside Trace.

Just then, the swing doors opened, and a younger man with a shock of red hair and a dark leather waistcoat over a deep blue shirt strode out, pushing a woman in front of him, before shoving her down to her knees. From the voluminous, high-class dress she wore, Trace figured she might be one of the performers from the Playhouse.

Trace wondered if this meant that Gilligan was also on the Rattler's payroll—as this Clay Slade had already attacked the mayor for his Rattler affiliations.

"Listen up, Colorado City!" the man hollered, shoving the woman in front of him as he held her by the back of the neck.

"I know you're down there! And I know you're sneaking about, wondering just what you are going to do about a guy like me!" the man shouted.

"Hopefully shoot him," Cephas whispered.

"My name is Clay Slade, and I don't care who hears it!" he hollered, as the woman at his feet whimpered.

"You got a problem, Colorado! You got a *big* problem! And you know what that is—the Rattler! So let me and my boys help you out some!" Clay laughed. Trace could tell he was lying.

"You give my boys the town—and we'll get rid of that dried-up has-been for you. And don't say we won't be fair. Every business will pay us and only us, and every ranch clears their deeds by us. That's fair for a bit of peace of mind, isn't it?" Clay shouted.

"Never!" Jackson shouted back, and at once, one of the guards standing beside Clay wheeled on his hips and snapped a shot off towards them. Trace grabbed the sheriff and pushed him back, but the shot went wide anyway and hit the wall of the building next to which they were crouching.

They weren't sharpshooters, Trace saw at once.

"You don't want to be saved? You don't want to save a beautiful woman like this one?" Clay laughed and thumped the end of his pistol against the crying woman's head.

Things were heating up fast. Trace could see that this Clay was a young, full-of-himself firebrand. He's probably made a successful outlaw out there on the trails, where his bravado and aggression would get him what he wanted. He probably thought he was good at what he did.

143

But all of that made him more dangerous. Not less. A man who didn't know his own limits was a man who would get in over his head—and would panic. Trace knew he had to nip this in the bud quickly, before something went very, very wrong.

"Buy some time!" Trace hissed and quickly outlined his plan to the sheriff before he took off up the street, behind the building.

"Trace! Where are you going?" Harlan hissed at him.

"Stay here! Wait for my signal!" Trace said, hurrying down the side street.

"What signal?" He heard Harlan hiss back—but Trace didn't have time to respond. He would just have to trust that Harlan would know it when he heard it.

"Alright! We'll talk! But we need time—we need to get the mayor down here..." Sheriff Jackson called from behind him. Clay answered back, but Trace was already too far away to hear it.

It was all about time now. Sometimes, success came down to seconds. Trace sprinted, turning down the side alley between two of the warehouses and ran for all he was worth. He skidded near the end, pausing to peer down the far side...

And to see just what he wanted.

The back of the playhouse was looking right at him, and it was a larger building than the saloon next to it. Trace could see a collection of wagons and hear the stamps of horses on the far side of the building where the saloon stood, but as yet, there were no gang members guarding the saloon.

"Let's hope I got this right..." Trace jogged down to the back door of the playhouse, his rifle in one hand as he turned the door handle.

Miracles upon miracles—it was unlocked.

Trace pushed the door open with his knee and aimed his rifle into the darkened room beyond.

It was dusty in there, and with a scent like grease paint and hemp. It appeared to be without any windows, and there were the shadows of boxes, crates, and barrels littered around the room, which Trace guessed were probably props and equipment for the stage shows that were put on.

He couldn't hear anything. No shouts, and no screams. He crept forward. The gang *must* have come through here to grab the showgirls, mustn't they? Didn't they think to post guards?

Trace crept through the storeroom to where a set of stairs led up to a narrow corridor, where a hazy, dusty light filtered through from outside.

It was then that Trace heard the first voice, a man's grunt from down the hallway. Trace froze, his rifle pointed at the corridor opening. There was a creak from the wooden floorboards, but nothing more.

Moving quickly, Trace slipped to the shadow beside the steps and, for a moment, fumbled in his pocket until he found a dime. He threw it onto the floor of the storeroom and waited.

"*Hgnh?*" There was a confused-sounding cough, and then the sound of boots hurrying to the stairs, and the form of a large man creaked down the steps.

Trace stepped out of the darkness and pressed the muzzle of his rifle into the side of the man's cheek.

"Shh!" Trace whispered.

The outlaw's eyes rolled, and Trace felt the man flinch, but he grinned and shook his head.

"How many?" Trace hissed under his breath, and when the man didn't say anything, Trace jammed the rifle harder into his cheek. "How many?"

The man hesitantly raised a hand, with only one finger raised.

"Good. Now get some of that rope. Now!" Trace waited until he bent down to pick up the rope, and then he smacked him hard on the back of the head with the butt of his rifle. He went out like a light.

Trace stripped him of his pistol, took his ammo belt and strapped it over his own, and then went back to the stairs, which he avoided by hopping lightly to the corridor itself.

The corridor appeared to stretch along the length of the building and led directly into the stage area on the right, as there were doors all along it. But Trace wasn't heading right. He walked slowly, purposefully down the corridor, hoping to imitate the guards' footsteps as he neared the only door on the left—the one that would lead into the saloon bar.

He was almost at it when a shape appeared out of the doors from his right with a wine bottle in one hand and a pistol in the other.

Trace had no time to surprise him, or to yell freeze. He launched himself forward, his rifle up as the outlaw swung his gun towards him.

Trace had no choice. He pulled the trigger.

The sound of his rifle going off in the corridor was thunderous, and the bottle exploded where the man clutched it to his chest. He was sent reeling back—and suddenly Trace was running for the saloon door.

"What's that? Where's Ford?"

Trace heard shouts as he slid to a crouch by the door and popped his rifle around the frame.

The door led straight into the saloon's back room. Four girls screamed where they sat on the floor, with just one outlaw guarding them. Trace's next bullet took that man down as he turned his gun toward Trace, and then Trace was springing forward.

"It's clear! Go-go-*go!*" he yelled to the girls, running past them as he heard shouts.

"We're under attack!"

Trace had almost gotten to the open archway that led into the main saloon lounge when gunshots started up outside. The sheriff had acted on his plan perfectly, opening fire as soon as he heard Trace's attack.

But right now, two outlaws were springing into the back room after him. Trace's final shot took one off his feet, and then he ducked to one side as the injured man fired. Trace spun around, using his momentum to turn his rifle into a bat that hit the second man in the stomach, before clubbing him over the back of the head.

Trace jumped back as bullets tore into the walls around him.

"He's right there! Get him!" Clay shouted.

Trace could see that his gang was just as pinned down as he was. Sheriff Jackson, Cephas, and Harlan were leading the barrage, and within seconds, all of the windows were smashed, and the gang was taking refuge behind whatever tables and chairs they could find.

Trace started firing, and not caring if he aimed or not. The point was to overwhelm, and quickly, not to kill. He dropped

147

his rifle and instead took out the stolen pistol and fired both into the room, to force the gang to keep their guns down.

"It's over, Clay! You're never getting out of this!" Trace shouted.

"Oh yeah? So I guess you don't mind if someone dies, huh?" Clay responded. There was a scandalized woman's scream as Clay Slade grabbed the same woman he had been holding hostage as before, and started to push her in front of him.

"You let me go, or else she gets it!" Clay screamed.

Trace winced. He had taken refuge by the door that led back into the saloon, and he had his pistols pointed at Clay's moving form.

"You're never going to get out of here, Clay. We got you surrounded. Just give it up and maybe you'll survive!" Trace hollered back. He wondered how many of the gang members he had already taken out. He knew he had shot two and injured two more. A further one was bleeding on the floor where the sheriff's men had shot him.

"How about the rest of you? You going to die for this creep?" Trace hollered at the rest of them. "We know he's the one behind all this. Drop your guns now, and we can cut a deal."

"*Don't any of you DARE!*" the man shouted—but there were only three gang members remaining.

One by one, each of them threw their guns onto the floor and held their hands up.

"Jackson!" Trace yelled, stepping forward to level his pistols on Clay, as the young gang leader looked wildly back and forth from his surrendering gang to Trace, who was almost standing over him.

"Give it up, Slade." Trace growled. "This was never going to happen on my watch. You picked the wrong town at the wrong time."

Trace saw the desperation and the fear in the outlaw's face. For a moment, he thought the man might do something stupid, but then he threw the woman ahead of him and dropped his pistol.

"Okay, okay—I get it. You're the big 'hoss around here. But you're really messing up. The Rattler is coming for this place, and you really should have asked for my help!" Clay Slade jeered.

"Shut up," Trace said, kicking the pistol out of the way as Sheriff Jackson, Harlan, and Deputy Cephas burst into the room, their guns sweeping everyone.

"He's all yours, Sheriff." Trace said wearily, as Jackson got to work.

The problem was, Trace knew that dealing with a young punk like Clay Slade was nothing compared to a wily old coyote like the Rattler.

Their problems as a town were only just beginning.

Chapter Seventeen

Cassidy Ranch, 1866

The house was quiet in the way that any ranch house generally was, and Annabelle heard the creaks and groans of the house as the wind pushed at its shingles and the old boards shifted in place.

The sound used to comfort her, when she heard it from her own ranch. The sound of the wind pushing against the shutters reminded her that she was safe, and warm, and surrounded by those she loved.

But that had all changed when the Rattler had come to her ranch. Now, Annabelle lay awake most nights, trying to hear if the wind hid the sound of a horse's rattle or a heavy boot. She had nightmares of smoke, billowing past curtains…

"It's all my fault," she whispered, pushing herself up from her bed and holding her head in her hands. Trace had gotten back the night before, and he had told them all of the attack on Colorado City by Clay Slade and his gang, and how the town had come together to defeat them.

But—when pressed—he had admitted that the town was lucky that there had only been eight of them, and that they were inexperienced. Trace was too honest for his own good, sometimes. As Harlan, Frankie, and old man Sawyer had congratulated him for a job well done—Annabelle remembered sitting there in shock.

They know that the Rattler is going to be ten times worse than that.

The Rattler wasn't just some young, half-drunk, half-mad pup looking to make some easy money. No—the Rattler had been the thorn in the side of Colorado for almost as long as Annabelle could remember. He was barely even a man in her mind; he was a nightmare, and a *demon*.

Harlan had told her that people were starting to leave the city, and almost a third of the ranches all around Pikes Peak had either been forced out or had just upped and abandoned their lands.

No one wanted to be here for what was coming, and now, when Annabelle listened to the wind, it didn't sound comforting; it sounded like a rising storm that was going to sweep them all away. If she didn't do something about it, that was.

Her hands went to the pillow on her bed, to the crumpled envelope underneath it—the one that she had found underneath her window, after it had slipped through the crack in the glass the other night.

Dearest Annabelle,

The time has come. I know that you can feel it too, and that is why I know that you cannot deny that we are destined to be together. I saw it in you that night when we first met. I saw your fire and I saw your courage—and I know that you saw the same in me.

You are to be mine, and together, we are going to remake Colorado territory. It is your destiny to be at my side.

There is only one sin in this world, and that is denying what you are and what you are destined to be. If you commit this sin, then know that everyone you have ever loved will be punished for standing in the way. Your friends, the Cassidys, and the

Daggers. You were never made for the poor likes of them anyway. You were made for me.

I will destroy this town and every ranch in the area if you do not give yourself to me, and you know that I can do it. History is on my side.

So, you will do the right thing. You will come to the old Casement Ranch. You have until the full moon, or else the town and your friends will pay.

With deepest affection,

The Rattler.

Annabelle scrunched the letter in her fist and felt an angry sob rise in her chest. Had it really come to this? Was this the only way she could save her friends? That she could save Trace?

The thought of Trace Cassidy made her heart want to break. He had come back from the war changed and hardened, but she knew that, underneath it all, there was still the wild, brave, carefree boy that she had loved.

Loved. Had she really just said that to herself?

"Yes," she whispered, as a tear rolled down her cheek. She had loved him then, back before she'd even had a word for what love was.

Annabelle raised her head. Then really, there was no answering it. She knew exactly what she had to do if she wanted to keep the people she loved safe.

She stood up and reached for her clothes.

***

The rain pelted down hard, like needles hitting her skin as she rode Prince through the storm. It felt like the weather was perfectly matching her decision, and the entire world was mourning with her.

Or it was angry. Maybe the entire world was as angry as she felt.

The land she had traveled was rough and uneven. There were briars and shrubs, and the grass was humped with ant mounds. It had once been a ranch, but the Casement family had abandoned it years ago.

Probably because of the Rattler, Annabelle thought bitterly.

Lightning split the sky, making Prince skitter, and Annabelle saw the silhouette of the rough, craggy hill nearby and a scatter of old ranch buildings.

And men on horseback, seated under one of the larger trees, with the cherry of a cigarette glowing in the dark.

"Hoi!" There was a shout, almost immediately snatched by the wind, and Annabelle slowed Prince down as the horse snorted and stamped. He didn't like being out in this weather, and she wondered whether he, too, could tell what she was doing.

"It's going to be alright, Prince," she said, slipping off the saddle and turning him around, back towards home.

"Go on. Go! *Go,* boy." She slapped his hind and he jumped forwards a few steps, before trotting to a stop to look back at her.

"GO!" Annabelle yelled, clapping her hands, and Prince suddenly broke into a prancing run.

He didn't deserve the life he would have with the Rattler, she thought.

"Hands up!" One of the two riders was moving towards her, barely controlling his horse in the storm. He managed to wheel the horse around and level his pistol at her.

"Oh!" The man looked startled, and under his hat, Annabelle recognized the tall, square jaw of the one who had come to ruin Frankie's wedding.

"Y'know what, lady—I did not expect that you would actually do it," he muttered, before gesturing with his gun to raise her hands.

"As if I had any choice," Annabelle said bitterly, as the man checked her over for guns.

"And there's no one with you? You sure?" The Rattler's righthand man said heavily, his eyes scanned the ground behind Annabelle, but it was impossible to see anything in this weather. He grumbled and wiped the rain from his eyes.

"No one. I know what the Rattler wants," Annabelle said heavily.

The lieutenant surprised her by sucking in the air as if shocked. A grimace crossed the man's face, but then he looked down at the drenched woman before him.

"You had a chance, you know. You could have stayed on that horse and kept riding. But I guess you didn't." He grunted before gesturing for her to get onto his horse. "The boss is going to be mighty pleased, is all I can say."

Annabelle said nothing at all. She felt her heart harden. She was doing this for her friends.

She was doing this for Trace.

The gang had clearly made an attempt to clean up the ranch buildings, and even rebuild most of them, and the fences around the main yard had been reinforced with long planks of wood, making it look more like a fort than an abandoned ranch. She heard a catcall from the open door of one of the barns and saw the movement of figures in the dark.

A low whistle from the other side of the yard alerted her to another outlaw, trying to stay dry under the sagging porch as the lieutenant rode up to it.

"I'm Briggs. You might as well know my name, as we're going to be seeing a lot of each other," he said.

Annabelle scoffed. "I don't care what your name is. You're a brute. Just like the rest of them."

The man shifted in his seat and then almost threw her to the ground with a snarl before jumping off his saddle himself.

"See to the horse!" Briggs barked at the other guard before grabbing one of Annabelle's arms and almost dragging her to the door.

"Boss! Boss—I got her!" he shouted loudly.

Annabelle blinked away the rain and tried not to show any sign of pain from Briggs' painful grip or fear about what she knew was coming. Instead, she tried to focus on her surroundings.

The Casement ranch house must have once been grand, and she was sure she remembered her father saying that the family had been one of the first to strike gold in the area—before the vein they had been hoping for turned out to be nothing more than a trickle, and all of their grand plans and dreams floundered.

But still, she could see how once the Casements had believed they had money, at least. The ranch house had a grand central staircase, and what looked like openings into dining rooms or even ballrooms on either side of the central hallway. There were discolorations on the wood-paneled walls, where presumably oil paintings had once sat. But the grandeur was long gone, and the hallway smelled of mildew and dust.

"Ahh. I knew you would come." A deep baritone voice rumbled from the gallery of the first floor. A figure strode to the top of the stairs and stood, holding an oil lamp in one hand.

Annabelle saw the flickering orange light over the Rattler's deep crimson and purple gown, and the way that it cast his dark hair and deep, sunken eyes into relief, making him look like a creature from her nightmares.

She couldn't help it. She struggled then, but Briggs' grip only tightened as he brought her up the stairs, using two hands this time to grab her other hand and set her in front of the Rattler.

The Rattler was a broad man, and older than she remembered him. Annabelle wondered if he was more than twice her age.

"You see it, don't you? You know that you and I were always destined to be together," the Rattler drew the words out.

Annabelle spat in his face. She might have to do this, but it didn't mean she had to be meek and mild.

"Ha! See, Briggs? That is just why she is the one!" The Rattler chuckled before taking a silk handkerchief from his pocket and cleaning the spittle from his face.

"Take her to her room." The Rattler dismissed her, and Briggs snarled as he pushed and shoved Annabelle down the gallery to one of the doors, kicking it open for Annabelle to see a simple bed. Suddenly, Briggs forced her down onto the bed and grabbed something that was lying underneath it. A coil of rope.

"Wait " Annabelle said, but before she could argue, Briggs had grabbed her hands and looped them hard, before tying them to the bed posts.

"This is what you asked for," Briggs said bitterly, standing up quickly and looking at her with wide eyes.

A shadow crossed the door to the bedroom, and the Rattler appeared once more.

No. Fear took over Annabelle then. She hadn't imagined it like this. This is not what she thought the Rattler wanted...

"Go," The bandit chief said to his second, and Briggs cast one more look at Annabelle before he vanished through the doorway.

"Finally," the Rattler smiled. "Now that I have you, I can begin. I will dismantle the town, piece by piece, ranch by ranch. Everyone who isn't *useful* to the Rattlesnake Free State will have to be removed."

"What are you talking about?" Annabelle looked at him. She had guessed that he was crazy, but now she was starting to think that this was something much worse even than that.

The Rattler wasn't just wild and dangerous; he sounded utterly insane.

He ignored her question, to stand and lecture her as if she were nothing but a child. "But first, of course, I will have to do something about that soldier of yours. Trace Cassidy. He has proven himself difficult, and I cannot have him confusing things for you, can I?"

"No," Annabelle whispered in horror. "You promised. In your letter, you promised no one would get hurt if I came here!"

"Promises are for children. Not for leaders, Annabelle. I was sure that someone of your caliber already knew that." The

Rattler leaned forward and brushed the back of his knuckles against her cheek.

"No! *No-no-no!*" Annabelle screamed and kicked her feet against the bed, against the frame, and the wall.

The Rattler, meanwhile, was chuckling as he stood up and walked to the door. "You will see, Annabelle. Once Trace Cassidy is dead, your mind will be clearer." He laughed again, as he swept out of the bedroom, leaving Annabelle to scream and shout—as there was a heavy thump, and a click as he locked the heavy door behind him.

Chapter Eighteen

Cassidy Ranch, 1866

"Annabelle!"

Trace hollered her name again into the gloomy woods, only to hear the mocking reply of birds, stirred up by his shout.

It was the next morning—almost midday by now—and Annabelle was still nowhere to be found. Trace waded through the bushy undergrowth to the clearing in the woods where he had found her the first time she had run off—the same clearing that they had both thought was entirely their own.

Water dripped from the leaves, and the upper branches of the trees still trembled with the dregs of last night's storm. The clouds up there were still heavy and gray, but Trace didn't notice them, nor the cold and damp.

There was a fallen tree in the center of the clearing, but Annabelle was not on it. She was not on the other side of it, and although it was almost impossible to tell after last night's gales, he couldn't see any sign that any animal larger than a mouse had been here recently.

Had the Rattler gotten her?

Trace shook his head, and his hat spat water droplets around him as he snarled in frustration. No. It couldn't be. Annabelle must have just ridden out early somewhere...

He did a quick circuit of the clearing, peering into the shadowy eaves to make sure there was no sign of her. Trace had been up early, as the soldier in him knew how to do. It had been the grays of pre-dawn when he had first gone out to check the gates and the animals.

And Prince had been gone. So was his saddle and his riding tack. At once, Trace had taken Bella to ride over to the Flint residence—but Sawyer, who was keeping an eye on the place, hadn't seen her that day.

That left the city—although Trace had made it abundantly clear that anywhere that Annabelle went, he wanted to go with her. Especially to Colorado City.

Trace had ridden hard to the sheriff's office and the general stores, but no one had seen Annabelle Flint there, either.

"These woods are my last chance." Trace muttered to himself. He spat on the ground, his face twisting in a snarl of desperation. He didn't want to admit even to himself that there was only one other reason for Annabelle's strange disappearance, wasn't there?

The Rattler.

"But why would she take her horse?"

He turned, jogging back through the woods to where he had tethered Bella outside. The wind caught at the prairie grasses, turning the plains into a wild sea. With a whistle, he had jumped onto his horse and wheeled her round—setting off in a gallop back to the farmhouse.

There was every chance that Annabelle was back at the Cassidy ranch, wasn't there?

Just what had she gone and done?

The rain was starting up by the time that he had come back, and he saw Frankie step out onto the kitchen porch to look up at him in alarm.

"Brother? Annabelle isn't with you?"

Trace felt his heart turn as cold as the rain that fell down the back of his neck. He stamped Belle to a stop, spattering mud and wet everywhere in the yard.

"So she's not here?"

"No." Frankie's face dropped. "I thought she was out with you."

Trace shook his head, jumping off his horse and barely waiting to lash her to the railing before he jumped inside. For once, Frankie didn't shout at him to take off his muddy boots as he barged into the house.

Harlan stood by the kitchen table, already pulling his jacket on, with a finished breakfast plate sitting on the side table. The younger man looked up, concern clear across his face. "Trace— I've already checked the range—she's not with the animals, and there's no sign she's been in the barns..."

"Apart from the stables. She took Prince." Trace said curtly, storming past him. Even though he knew she wasn't there, he still swung into the living room to see if she had miraculously appeared there, and the smaller store pantry, before taking the stairs three at a time.

He heard Harlan start to holler a question behind him, but Frankie quickly shushed him. He didn't hear what his sister was urgently saying, and right now he didn't care.

She wasn't upstairs. She wasn't in Trace, Frankie, or Harlan's rooms or in the small loft space.

"Annabelle!" Trace called out, unable to contain himself.

There was only one place left, where she hadn't been this morning when Trace had checked. And surely Frankie would have checked several times over already this morning—but Frankie had to see with his own eyes.

Annabelle *had* to be in her room. Because the only other option was too awful.

Trace clattered back down the stairs to where the spare bedroom sat at the back of the house, its door still open where he had left it. He marched in, turning around to see the exact same sight he had seen in the early hours of this morning.

Nothing. The bed was made. Her most recent blouse was folded on top of the clothes desk, and her hairbrush was beside it. Nothing was out of the ordinary, and yet everything was totally wrong.

"The window," Trace murmured, moving at once to where the shutters were still closed. He threw the latch and flung the shutters open to see that the window was still closed, but he rattled it for good measure. One of the window jams was a little loose, allowing a sliver of air through.

Not the window. It hadn't been broken, and it hadn't been forced. So Annabelle couldn't have been kidnapped... Trace was at a complete loss for where she was. He spun on his heel...

...just as something scrunched against his sliding foot and scattered across the floor.

It was a crumple of paper, left on the floor by the side of the bed.

Annabelle wasn't generally an untidy person, Trace thought. The folded sheets and the carefully arranged hairbrush said as much.

He stooped down to grab the piece of paper, opening it to see that it was a letter written in broad black script. His brow furrowed as he read the first few lines.

Oh no.

***

"She's gone to *him!*" Trace hissed as soon as he stepped back into the kitchen. He brandished the letter that the Rattler had written to Annabelle, half torn across the middle.

"What?" Harlan gasped.

"Oh goodness. Of course she has," Frankie whispered, dropping herself into one of the kitchen chairs and her head falling into her hands.

Anger flared through Trace. How could he have been so blind? "Did you know? Did anyone know?" he shouted, thumping the piece of torn paper on the table and turning to pace rapidly through the kitchen.

"Of course I didn't know, Trace. I would have tied her to that chair if I did!" Frankie said irritably and miserably. She picked up the letter and spent a few moments reading it before passing it on to Harlan.

"But of course she did. She loves this place. She loves *us*, Trace." Frankie's voice was earnest, and he heard her chair scrape as she turned to look at him.

Trace remained resolutely staring out of the open back door. He couldn't meet his sister's eyes right now.

"She would do anything to protect us all. You know that too, brother," Frankie said softly, and it made Trace's heart break.

"But not this!" He finally turned around, feeling a big ball of rage and tumult in his chest. *What did Annabelle think she was doing? How could she leave them? Did she really think that the Rattler would spare anyone if she gave herself to him?*

"I know." Frankie rose from her chair and moved to put a wary hand on Trace's shoulder. He shrugged it off.

"No. This isn't happening. Not on my watch. I'm going to find her, and I'm going to get her back," he swore.

"You will." Frankie nodded sagely.

Behind them, Harlan shifted where he stood. His face was full of foreboding. "I think it must have had the address here once, but see? That part has been torn off. Maybe Annabelle took it with her to find it."

"Or she thought she was keeping us safe by not knowing," Frankie pointed out.

Trace once again ignored her searching look. He had no time for questions. What he needed now was action. He had already made up his mind, and he turned towards the door.

"Brother! Where are you going?" Frankie started after him.

But Trace didn't stop. "You two stay here and keep an eye on the trails. Get your rifles. I'm going to town and I'm going to put a stop to the Rattler for good."

Chapter Nineteen

Calico Pass, Western Colorado, 1866

"This is the place?" Trace growled, shooting a glance over his shoulder at the very pale face of Mayor Keeley, seated on his horse beside him.

The sun was only just rising over the hills, and ahead of them sat a small stand of trees, with the edge of an old peaked barn visible on the far side. Ivy and creepers clung to its walls and had almost entirely reclaimed it.

"It is," the mayor, still injured and still recovering, rasped. There was a clip from behind him, as Sheriff Jackson rode into view, along with Cephas and a dozen other deputies and willing men from the city.

It was late afternoon of the next day by the time the sheriff had managed to raise enough men. They had talked to the mayor almost at once, as Trace knew that Keeley had at least some connection to the Rattler (however hard he tried to deny it), and the mayor had given them this place, the old Cottleshom barn.

"I'll lead," Trace said at once, slipping off his horse and handing the reins to Mayor Keeley, despite the fact that Keeley looked positively terrified.

"Maybe this is what you should have encouraged the sheriff to do years ago." Trace growled as he pressed the reins into Keeley's hands. Trace was disgusted. How many lives could have been saved if the mayor had decided to trust his community rather than abandon them?

165

"How do you want to play this?" Sheriff Jackson asked, easing himself to the ground at the same time and checking his gun belts.

They had twelve assorted deputies and upstanding folks from Colorado with them, including Harlan. Trace had asked that Sawyer stay close to Frankie. Trace saw a sea of wary— some scared—but mostly defiant faces. The men had brought a range of rifles or sidearms.

This was a moment for a speech, but Trace didn't know what to say. He was a scout, not a general.

"Let's get our people back." Trace murmured, earning a ripple of agreeing grunts and solemn faces.

Trace divided them into three groups with four people in each. Harlan with one group, the sheriff with another, and Trace with the third. Using hand signals, he indicated that Harlan was to go around the back while the sheriff should hang back before heading to the front of the barn.

And he would lead his three other men straight through the woods, directly to the barn itself.

"Stay low. You don't stop until you get to the tree cover, even if they start firing," Trace hissed, breaking into a loping run through the long grasses as Harlan led his three on a wider arc towards the back of the woods, as well.

Trace had Cephas with him, as well as one of the feed merchants, and an older rancher from the other side of the city, who remembered the bad old days of the Rattler. All of them nodded as they ran and did their best to imitate Trace's movements.

They hit the tree line without a whisper of movement from the barn, which Trace thought was an excellent sign. Most bandits weren't especially known to be early risers, anyway.

Instantly, they were in the gloom of the trees, and Trace waved his hand for them to slow down as they picked their way past the brambles and vines, and weaved past the ghostly Birch trees. The first glimmers of the sun hadn't yet penetrated the small copse, and Trace was confident they wouldn't be seen until they stepped out at the far end.

There, through the trees, he could see the overgrown Cottleshom barn. It was only discernible by the fact that its moldering wood and greenery were angular, rather than natural.

There were several dark holes where windows should be, as well as one larger hole near the base that looked to Trace like a crawl hole. He crept towards the last tree and spied that there were broken bits of glass littered nearby.

Bandits and outlaws weren't known to be the tidiest bunch, either.

He slung his rifle off his shoulder and gestured for the others to spread along the tree line. It was strange to think of the Rattler choosing a place like this for his hideout. It looked almost ready to fall down, and Trace wondered just how ancient it was.

But the mayor had said that this was one of the Rattler's places, and this had been where Keeley had been summoned to meet with the man. Trace had seen that the front of the barn had wide doors, big enough to haul a stolen wagon or carriage in. Maybe that was what they used this place for.

He checked his rifle quickly, and when he knew that it was fit to his satisfaction, he raised up a little, and whistled in a surprisingly good imitation of an owl.

For a second, there was no sound, and then an answering hoot came by on the far side. Harlan was in place.

"Okay. Follow behind me. Don't fire unless I do!" Trace whispered to his men before he broke cover, sighting down his rifle as he stalked to the nearest window.

Those first steps over open ground felt like they lasted a lifetime—when in fact Trace crossed them in just a few moments. He reached the end of the barn and set his back to the wood, waiting for Cephas, the merchant, and the rancher to do the same along this side of the barn.

Pretty good! Trace thought that they might make passable scouts yet.

Moving as quietly as a shadow, he turned and presented his rifle to the window, his eyes following the glimmers of golden-dawn light and trying to discern what was in the shadows.

Humped shapes. Old barrels. Decaying bags.

What?

He couldn't see Annabelle. In fact, he couldn't see anyone.

There was a shift of movement in the dark, and Trace's rifle flickered to one side at once, to see something move. A body! A form rolled over.

Gotcha!

Trace stepped back, signaling to the others to wait as he ran to the crawl hole, his heart swelling as he ducked through. Perhaps they had been unbelievably lucky. Perhaps the rest of the outlaws had gone out somewhere, and they had left Annabelle behind? Or perhaps this was a guard who could tell them where Annabelle was!

He ducked into the barn to instantly smell the earthy smell of moss and mold. He rose slowly, letting his eyes adjust until he saw the shapes of old crates and discarded hessian sacks.

And a figure—a man—half lying under sacks and groaning as he yawned awake.

"Don't move!" Trace hissed at once and leveled his rifle straight at the waking man.

"*Hgnh!?*"

Trace stepped forward so that the man could see him—and more importantly, see the gun.

"*Huh!?*"

The man shifted, blinking in the dawn light, and Trace's heart suddenly plummeted. He knew this figure. This man was older than when he had last seen him, but he didn't look as though he had changed that much in his habits.

It was old Ellijah, the city drunk. He was no outlaw and certainly no bandit. He wandered around the city, begging for pennies to feed his booze, and when they ran out, he would be found in people's ranch barns and stables all around here, occasionally stealing some eggs if he was feeling quick enough.

It was obvious that old Elijah had chosen the Cottleshom barn as a dry place to spend a windy night, and nothing more.

"What did I do? I didn't mean it—whatever it was!" old Elijah almost shrieked in fright.

"You haven't seen a group of men about here? With Annabelle Flint?" Trace slowly lowered his gun, but kept his tone severe.

"Who? Flint? The young lady—no! I haven't seen her for months now! No one here but me, sir, I promise you!" old Elijah said, and Trace believed him.

Unfortunately, that meant that they still had absolutely no idea where Annabelle was.

***

It was a bust. Trace gritted his teeth behind his kerchief as he rode back towards the ranch, with Harlan at his side. The afternoon was drawing late, and he didn't remember the last time he ate, but he didn't feel tired. If anything, he felt like lightning was slowly burning through his body.

"They weren't at the barn, and no one at the saloons knows anything about where they are," Harlan growled beside Trace, voicing their shared frustration. "How can no one know where the Rattler is? He's been in the area for years!"

"He's had ten years to dig himself in," Trace responded. "Either that, or the people who know are too scared to say."

"Like Mayor Keeley?" Harlan asked. He looked away when he saw Trace's dark look.

If that man wasn't already shot... Trace just managed to rein in his words. He was at a loss. None of the local ranchers knew where the Rattler could be. And they had even sent a telegram to the Denver Sheriff's Office, in case anyone up there had better intelligence.

A small spurt of dust on the horizon drew Trace's attention. As he squinted against the sun, he saw there was a rider, drawing away from a couple of trees and starting to ride away from them, fast.

"Harlan. Anyone brought that piece of land over there? I thought that was the Price's?" Trace said.

"It is. But their cattle are up on the other side of the rise. I know because one of their ranch hands was in our posse," Harlan said.

"Then what is a rider doing out there?" Trace gritted his teeth. That way led to nowhere that he knew of. The nearest creek was in their direction, not his.

And the man was riding *fast*—just like what a scout would do once they had confirmed eyes on a target.

"Drat!" Trace suddenly realized what was going on.

"Trace?" Harlan looked at him in shock.

"The nearest ranch to here is *ours*. And no one has any business being out there unless they're working. That was a spy, Harlan—I promise you."

"Frankie!" The name burst out of Harlan, and the younger man threw his steed forward, breaking into a gallop as fast as he could.

The pair tore over the prairie, their steeds eating up the distance between them and home. There was no smoke. Nothing was on fire. All that met them was the smell of braising beef.

"Frankie, my heart! Frankie!" Harlan yelled as Sawyer came jogging out of the nearby barn, his rifle in one hand.

"Son! What in the blazes is happening?"

"Wait, nothing is happening here? You haven't seen anyone?" Harlan said, as Trace pulled up Bella and looked suspiciously around the yard. Everything seemed exactly where it should be.

"We saw a rider heading in this direction. Or keeping an eye on the trail between the ranch and the city," Trace explained, as Frankie came out in her apron, her sleeves rolled up and a pistol in one hand.

"You didn't find her?" Frankie's first words were a plea.

"No." Trace shook his head abruptly. "But we have to be careful. We *all* have to be very careful. I don't think the Rattler has given up at all. I think he's keeping an eye on all of us…"

He and Harlan dismounted, and they recounted their failed attempts and lack of faith in the mayor as they brought their horses to the stables. Trace felt a dark cloud over his thoughts. He wanted to get back out there. Perhaps he could even track that rider they had seen—but Frankie and Sawyer insisted that he at least eat for now, and going out alone would just endanger them all.

Trace didn't like it, but he saw the sense in eating at least, even if he knew that all food would be tasteless without Annabelle here.

I'm in love with her, he admitted to himself as he allowed himself to be led back to the house. He thought about the half-crazed girl she had been, always laughing, and as quick as a jumping fish.

I have always been in love with her, ever since the start.

It didn't feel strange to admit this, as he sat through their evening meal and chewed on the meat that was probably delicious—just not to him.

They were still eating at the kitchen table when there was a shout and a clatter of hooves from outside in the yard. Trace immediately jumped up and was the first to get to the door. He flung it open to see that Sheriff Jackson and Cephas were riding into their yard, looking flustered.

"It's the Rattler!" Sheriff Jackson gasps. "He attacked saloons and stores all across town this afternoon—throwing bricks through windows and shooting people dead when they ran out. He shouted that Colorado City was *his!*"

Trace knew it. This was exactly what he had guessed would happen. The Rattler didn't want any singular person. He wanted everything. And he wasn't going to stop until he got it.

Chapter Twenty

Western Colorado Territories, 1866

Annabelle woke up, and it was the wrong time.

It should be daytime, only it wasn't. The shutters were still closed, but there was no tell-tale crack of light coming from between the jamb.

How long did I sleep? She tried to move, and suddenly her wrist hurt and she struggled to remember why. Had she broken it? Had the Rattler hurt her? No—not that she could remember.

It was then that her eyes focused and she saw the thick hessian rope that was secured around her wrist, leading to the bed frame itself.

"Oh, right," she remembered. She was tied up. To the bed. Just like she had been the same time she had woken before...and hadn't that been night time as well?

She felt woozy as she tried to sit up—or the best that she could do in the circumstances, with one arm tied to the bed. She had worked out that she could get into a lean that at least changed her position for a while, until that started hurting too.

"My thoughts..." Annabelle murmured to herself. She was still so very sleepy, and her muscles felt heavy and leaden.

He's drugging me with something, isn't he?

Annabelle had never had opium in her life, not even when she had once broken her wrist, falling off some rocks. She had spent the summer in a splint that Doctor Kilgore had come out and changed every month, applying tight bands that had made her eyes water. But she had never had the opium, and so she couldn't say if that was what she was feeling now.

There was a sudden blare of candlelight as the door opened, and in walked the old woman—the one that Annabelle remembered had been looking after her these last few days. She had a bowl of something hot and a pitcher of water.

"Oh, good, you're awake," the older woman croaked, and her voice was like sandpaper. She had hair that was more gray than it was white—and though it might have once been held in a bun, it was more like a ragged mop. Her long dress looked old and had been restitched many times.

"Who are you?" Annabelle asked again, and she recollected that this was not the first time she had asked this woman to help.

A worried look crossed the woman's features as she set the pitcher down on the floor and pursed her lips for a moment.

"Best you don't know my name, girly. It'd only get us both in trouble." The older woman heaved a sigh and set herself down on the floor beside the bed before lifting the pitcher up for her prisoner to drink from.

Annabelle gulped at the water greedily, and then instantly felt ashamed of being grateful for it. She should spit it out, and refuse to eat, and scream that she wasn't going to do anything that the Rattler ever wanted.

But that wouldn't help, would it? Annabelle thought a little more clearly as she took her fill of water. The Rattler was an evil, controlling man. The more she fought against him, the more he appeared to delight in adding little punishments in the form of skipped meals or tighter ropes.

And the more trouble I am in, the greater the chance he will take it out on Trace!

A sob tore through her chest then, and it wasn't just at her own condition. It was a fact that the only people she really loved were out there somewhere, and that there was nothing she could do to protect them.

"Nothing apart from being in here. With *him,*" she murmured to herself.

There was an intake of breath from the old woman, who set her palm to Annabelle's face and shushed her. It was the closest thing that Annabelle had felt to tenderness in what felt like a long time.

"Oh, you're so young. So very young," the old woman whispered gently. Annabelle saw the woman's face harden. "Too young for this. I'm old now, and when the Rattler killed my husband to take the ranch, there was no way I could fight back. But you..."

"I can't," Annabelle whispered. "If I fight, he might kill those I love outside."

The older woman's eyes were kind. "You have a sweetheart? Someone on the outside?"

Yes. Annabelle's heart leapt to Trace, to his strong jaw and his clear eyes, and to the way that he was like a wolf on a scent when he was passionate.

"I think so," she whispered. "I hope so."

The older woman appeared to think about that answer for a longer moment, nodding slowly to herself. After a moment, she turned, bringing the food to Annabelle's lap and setting a spoon in the bowl of what looked like a stew.

"Someone will rescue you. I know they will. I may even be able to get word out..."

She was busy whispering this when the door suddenly pushed open, and the looming form of the Rattler swept into the room.

"You—*out!*" he commanded the older slave woman at once, who flinched instinctively and scrambled out of the door.

The Rattler stood uncomfortably close to Annabelle, looking down at her as she gritted her teeth.

"Well? Aren't you going to eat? Do I not care for you?" he demanded.

He had come in here with the faint whiff of brandy on his breath, and looking for an argument. Annabelle was confused as to why he wanted to argue with her so much when he'd professed to loving her.

And if I anger him too much, he might kill Trace!

So Annabelle, very slowly, took the spoon and served herself some stew, before bobbing her head. She would try a new tack with the Rattler. Maybe silently ignoring him wasn't the way to get what she wanted.

"Thank you," she whispered.

"What?" The Rattler frowned at that. It was the first time she had said anything to him that wasn't a shout.

"Thank you for taking care of me. It is very kind," Annabelle said once again. "I—I have been doing some thinking..."

"Axel," the Rattler said, his voice in lowered tones. "Call me Axel." He seemed confused by her sudden change in attitude.

"I...I have decided that I will give myself to you... my heart, completely—if you promise me that you will spare Trace Cassidy, and all the Cassidys. And the Daggers."

"Trace Cassidy!" Axel suddenly recoiled as if struck. "The soldier? The boy?"

Annabelle saw his dark eyes spark with rage, and she suddenly realized that she had said the wrong thing. It was too soon for games with this man, and he was too drunk.

"This is still unacceptable! That soldier boy has twisted your mind! You are still in love with him, aren't you? Tell me the truth!" Axel snapped. He sounded mortified for some reason.

Annabelle opened and closed her mouth. What could she say? There was nothing that might not result in the death of the man she loved.

"I...I..."

"You are still addled. And clearly have much more thinking to do." Axel's face suddenly twisted in hate as he reached down to grab the bowl of stew and dashed it against the other side of the room. Annabelle flinched from the clatter—but there was no slap or blow following it.

"You are protecting him, and you haven't fully given your heart to me. But you will see the error of your ways, Annabelle Flint!"

The outlaw snarled, turning on his heel and marching out of the room, slamming the door behind him. Annabelle was left on the bed, with the memory of only one spoonful of stew. But she smiled to herself.

I can manipulate him. I know I can.

Maybe she could even use the power of her words to free herself.

Chapter Twenty-One

Cassidy Ranch, 1866

The lonesome howl of a coyote lifted over the prairie, and Trace shifted a little in his crouch.

It was a full night, with only a sliver of moon left to turn the grasses silvery and pale. Trace pulled his poncho a little tighter over his shoulders and cocked his head to listen a little deeper.

The flutter of moths. The cooing of night birds. A gentle breeze sighing over his land.

"Okay then." He slowly stood up, aware of how his joints had become stiff, and rolled his shoulders. He hadn't seen anyone out here yet, and the calls of the wild animals told him that the prairies hadn't been disturbed by intruders.

Not yet, anyway.

Still, Trace turned slowly, scanning the horizon once more for any signs of anything out of place. Nothing that the eyes of a trained scout could see.

But it didn't mean that the Rattler wasn't out there—and waiting.

With a barely controlled growl of frustration, Trace set off on the narrow track that led back to the ranch. It was another fruitless night of no word about the Rattler's gang—other than they had stepped up their attacks. There were attacks in the city. A barn had been burned down north of here. A mail carriage had been surrounded and shot out, forcing it to turn around.

"The Rattler's closing us off," Trace murmured to the wind. He hadn't brought Bella with him as he kept watch. He'd sacrificed speed for stealth.

With every passing hour, he could almost see the invisible grip of the Rattler closing around Western Colorado. If the Rattler succeeded in closing the main roads in, then he would effectively have control of everywhere up to the Colorado mountains.

But Trace knew he would have to take out the 'troublesome' ranches first—the ones that would fight back, no matter what.

Ranches like the Cassidys.

Trace lifted his head to his own buildings, silhouetted against the stars ahead of him. The Cassidy ranch was prominent in the landscape, with the main building in the center, then his main barn, little barn, and the stable block forming a small square. It stood alone for miles—but that also meant they had eyes all around. Any attackers would have to come up Little Creek if they wanted to remain hidden, and it was into the wooded incline of Little Creek that he now slipped.

This was the place where we swung over the stream. Trace saw the old willow tree with its spreading boughs. He thought of Annabelle as she had been, years ago, years before the war had come.

They had been happy, hadn't they?

Pain clutched at his heart, so strong that he had to pause and steady himself against the nearest tree.

Where was she? Where was Annabelle? What was happening to her right now?

The tumult inside was almost enough to unman him, but Trace pushed himself forward. A dull anger burned inside of him, waiting to flare up.

"Keep it together," he breathed to himself. He had let anger and revenge overcome him before, hadn't he? Trace remembered the terrible fury he had felt after Wade and Colt had died. He recalled the weight of the grenade in his hand.

He had been mad then; he knew now. But he was no longer that man.

This battle against the Rattler was not just about him. It was about the entire community, and the community of Western Colorado deserved justice.

"They've been scared for too long," Trace murmured. He thought of the scars that just about everyone around here bore thanks to the terror that the Rattler had inflicted over the years. While revenge would be sweet, it didn't make those scars go away.

The people need to see justice, he thought. They needed to see the Rattler's gang brought before the courts, and they needed to feel strong.

Yes. This realization felt right to Trace in a way that he had rarely felt over the last few years. He *loved* this place and this whole community with every fiber of his being. He knew that he was not only willing to fight for it—he was willing to help it heal as well.

He was so lost in his thoughts that he almost didn't register the crunch of leaves in the wooded creek. At once, he dropped into a crouch, his rifle coming up as he waited, sighting down the creek bed.

Trace felt his breathing slow, and his heartbeat was steady as he leaned into his rifle. His entire body was relaxed, as he allowed his senses to open. He heard the sigh of the wind in the branches above him and the gentle trickle of water.

Trace waited until he was sure that there was no answering crunch of leaves, and slowly, very slowly, stood back up.

The house! He had to get to the house. If that sound *had* been an intruder, then it might be one of the Rattler's scouts, coming to search for weak spots.

He ghosted out of the creek at the bottom of the lower paddock and silently moved towards the stables. He heard the soft snort of the horses inside. They weren't upset and stamping, so if the Rattler *had* sent a scout, they must be good. Very good.

He padded up the side of the stable to the main yard, to see the barn and the main ranch house standing just as they always had before. He waited for a pause longer, until he was sure that he couldn't hear any sounds of intruders, before crossing to the ranch building.

He couldn't hear any sound from inside the house, and both the front and back doors were still locked. The new shutters he had installed on the outside of all of the windows were still locked, and it looked as though the defenses that he had put in place were holding.

Maybe it was nothing, he thought—just before there was the distinct sound of a cough.

Trace spun on his heel, his rifle coming up and pointing down the main yard to see out there, stepping onto the main track was a figure.

Even from this distance and in the gloom of night, Trace thought he recognized something about his shape and the way he loped across the ground. The man wasn't making any attempt to hide himself, although Trace knew that he had been good enough to get this far undetected.

The figure paused on the road before he came up to the main yard and very, very slowly, he raised both of his hands in the air.

"He knows I am watching him," Trace whispered. Did that mean the man had accomplices?

Trace waited until the man had reached their end gate. "Whoa right there!"

There was still no sign of any other intruders, and the horses weren't stamping or making any noise. They were usually a good indication that there were other horses around, at least.

"Makes it kinda hard to talk, having to holler like that!" the man shouted.

Ice ran through Trace's veins. He knew that voice, and in that moment, he remembered who he was. It was the same man who had come to threaten them at Frankie and Harlan's wedding. It was one of the Rattler's own.

"Say your piece now, before I put some lead between your eyes!" Trace snarled. He thought he heard a gentle thump from inside the house, and the soft murmur of voices as Harlan or Frankie must have woken up.

He aimed at the man's legs. It was an old soldiering trick— tell them where you're aiming, but all the while be able to halt them before they jumped.

The man shifted where he stood, and Trace saw him nod.

"The name's Briggs. You may have heard of me," the man called out.

"Nope." Did this guy think that his name alone was going to frighten him? Trace didn't know or care who he was. He was working for the Rattler and was important enough to deliver messages.

"Look—Trace, isn't it? Trace Cassidy?" Briggs began.

"Where is she?" Trace interrupted him. He didn't have the patience for any 'friendly' banter from this thief. "Here's a message for you. The Rattler has to let Annabelle Flint go, safe and unharmed, and he has to leave Colorado. If he does this, then he might make it out of all this alive."

There was a soft snort of surprise from the man, who kicked some of the dust on the roadway. Trace heard the murmuring growing louder inside the house, and one of the upstairs windows—one of the ones that didn't have an external shutter just for this reason—opened, and a rifle slid out.

"*Trace?*" It was Harlan's tense voice.

"Not yet. Be ready." Trace hissed back, as Briggs cleared his throat to speak again.

"The thing is, Cassidy—I don't want any part of this. The Rattler has gone mad. I've come to offer you a deal."

You come to make a deal, huh? Trace narrowed his eyes. Did this outlaw expect him to just take his word for it?

"Is she unharmed! Tell me he hasn't touched her!" Trace shouted.

"He hasn't laid a finger on her. Not yet, anyway. He's saying all these things about how he wants a queen for his kingdom. He's obsessed with her," Briggs explained.

Trace felt sick at the words. They brought him little comfort indeed.

"And look. This is enough for me. I'm not working for a madman, and I have no interest in kidnapping women," Briggs continued. "I didn't join up to do that. I just want to make my money and get out of here. I don't need the sort of blood feuds this will bring."

Huh, Trace considered. *You have no idea.* Fury burned in Trace's heart. He was not going to stop until Annabelle was freed. Maybe Briggs knew that, too.

"So here's the deal," Briggs carried on. "I'll help you get your girl back. I'll tell you where she is and where the Rattler is and everything."

Trace couldn't hold onto it any longer. This man knew where Annabelle was. Briggs could have brought her here himself if he wanted to!

"Where is she! Tell me, darn it!" Trace hissed.

"Not so fast!" Briggs shouted back. "I need some assurances first, or you get nothing!"

Trace said nothing. He continued aiming at the man's legs.

"Me and my boys don't want to be guards for the Rattler's new kingdom. That's not what we're about. And we certainly don't want to work for any madman who'll just get us killed. So—we give you the girl, and you let the rest of us be. We'll hightail it out of this accursed territory. It doesn't even have any gold in it!" Briggs shouted. There was even a hint of desperation in his voice.

Trace saw what the man was. He wasn't a coward—he was just an outlaw, through and through. He wanted quick, violent raids with maximum profit. If the Rattler really was intending on trying to control a city, then the Rattler was asking them to become soldiers, not bandits.

And there is no way that I am going to let any of you walk free, Trace gritted his teeth. They had done too much harm. *Had Briggs been the one to burn down Annabelle's ranch? To shoot innocent people in the city? How many of these gang members had been there when his own parents had been killed?*

Nope. That was not something that Trace was going to let happen...but he didn't have to tell Briggs that, did he?

"You got a deal. Where?" Trace shouted back—and he heard a soft gasp from above him. Frankie must be with Harlan, listening to the whole proceedings.

"Tomorrow night, and you'll have your sweetheart. The old Lamberts' place."

The Lamberts'? Trace blinked, trying to remember it. He had a dim recollection of a family called the Lamberts. His pa had talked about them. But hadn't they already gone by then? Trace thought he remembered his father talking to old man Flint about how they had been one of the first to be driven out. But that must have been almost twenty years ago!

"What do you say, Cassidy? We got a deal? You want your woman back?"

She's not 'mine'. Trace threw the thought back, but he did bare his teeth possessively. Annabelle might not be anyone's—but he would still die to defend her.

"You got a deal," Trace said, and Briggs visibly sighed and let his hands down. He turned slowly around—heading for Little Creek, where presumably he must have hidden his horse. The bandit took about three steps before he spun back around towards Trace.

"And don't try anything smart, y'hear? Or you'll regret it!" Briggs sneered.

186

Trace didn't reply. He watched as Briggs loped off into the darkness, and within a few heartbeats, Trace couldn't even hear the sound of his feet.

Trace looked at the patch of shadow that Briggs had disappeared into, and promised himself that every one of the Rattler's gang would be brought to justice—every last one.

Chapter Twenty-Two

Cassidy Ranch, 1866

"Brother, *no.*" Frankie stood in front of him in the Cassidy kitchen and placed her fists on her hips.

It was morning by now, but their conversation hadn't got much further than this, as Trace sat at the table with his waxed roll displaying his available weapons as he cleaned them. Two rifles and two pistols, with both Harlan and Sawyer owning their own rifles as well.

He hoped it would be enough to both take on the gang, the Rattler, and to protect the ranch while he was away.

"What? We can do this, sister," Trace said, frowning as he inspected the guns again for any signs of dirt. There weren't any. They gleamed from the amount of machine oil he had worked into them.

"All we have to do is to get the sheriff and the posse to confront Briggs' gang, while I capture the Rattler. Briggs has pretty much admitted that he won't stand in the way of that," Trace explained. "And then Anna will be free!"

Frankie sighed sharply, turning to rub a hand over her temples before coming back to the table with a pot of coffee. She thumped it down in that way she had when she was annoyed.

"Briggs said that he wanted to *leave*. Let him do it! Then you don't have to endanger yourself. If you pick a fight with the Rattler *and* Briggs, then aren't you just adding trouble for yourself?" She paused, her hands shaking for just a moment.

Trace set the guns down and turned to her. His sister was angry—but underneath that, he could see that she was scared. First she had lost her brother, then her fiancé, and now Annabelle too. He could see that she didn't want to lose anything more.

"Frankie, this is *how* we keep us safe. And not just for now, or for tonight—but for the long haul," Trace said softly.

"Men like Briggs...I know them. I've met them before, in the war. Yes, he doesn't want to work for a madman like the Rattler—but I promise you that he will just as soon come back if a spot of gold is discovered," Trace said earnestly.

It wasn't that he hated Briggs. He didn't care one way or another about the man.

But he cared about justice. He searched for the words on how to tell his sister that enough was enough. Colorado had been at the mercy of gangs like the Rattler and Clay Slade for too long.

Colorado was a wild territory, barely recognized as such, but now with entire towns and cities inside it. There was word that the railway was going to start coming through one day—if they could clear the territory of its lawlessness.

"We all need to come together," Trace said in a softer voice, holding his hand out for his sister. Frankie looked subdued, but then crossed the kitchen floor to clasp his own briefly.

"Colorado deserves this. It deserves justice. We need to make a stand to say that we are not going to let outlaws and crooks and bandits ruin our lives, or ruin our streets anymore." Trace announced, and as soon as he said it, he felt the rightness of his words.

And they need to know they can never do this again. Trace's expression hardened.

189

"This isn't just about Colorado City, or even just about us. It's about everyone. What if Briggs ever decided to do the same somewhere out there to someone else? What if there is ever another Annabelle, or..." his voice trailed off before he could say Pa and Ma.

But Frankie nodded that she understood.

"I—I get it, Trace, I really do. I just wish that it wasn't so dangerous. I feel like everything has already been taken from me," Frankie whispered.

There was a soft cough from the kitchen door as Harlan stepped in from outside, his rifle in his hands.

"All clear," he whispered, before crossing at once to Frankie and enfolding her in his arms. He must have overheard their conversation, as he rubbed her back and murmured into her hair. "I'm not going anywhere, Frankie. I promise you, I'm not going anywhere."

Trace felt a stab of envy at that. Their bond was obvious, and the love they had for each other was clear. He wondered whether he would ever have such a thing...

And did Annabelle even think about him in the same way?

Trace blinked, looking at his sister and her husband, and he realized something. As much as it would hurt, as much as he might never recover if Annabelle didn't want him—he knew that his feelings would never change.

I'll still be here, and I will still protect her to my last breath.

In a strange way, Trace felt almost calm.

He was going to save Annabelle—and he was going to make sure that no one got away with the hurt they had caused the people of Colorado.

***

Annabelle couldn't stop herself from flinching when the door to her room opened suddenly, but she managed to plaster a hopeful smile on her face as Axel strode in.

"Axel." She greeted him and sat up.

She had no idea what time of the day it was, and she felt just as lethargic and slow as she had a couple of days ago—so she guessed that he was still drugging her food.

The bandit leader paused in the room, looking suspiciously down at her for a long moment, before he huffed through his nose and fumbled something from his pocket.

It was a bag of candies, frosted with powdery sugar icing. The outlaw said nothing as he offered her the bag, and Annabelle looked up at him.

Annabelle forced her smile a little wider. "Oh, thank you. It's been a time since I had any of those!" She reached up with her one free hand to the packet—and Axel's free hand shot out to grab her wrist suddenly.

"*Ach!*" The bandit's grip was like a vice. He squeezed her wrist like he wanted to break it.

"Axel—you're hurting me!" Annabelle murmured. She struggled to keep her smile, despite the fact that the bandit's grasp was getting stronger and stronger.

"Tell me you love me! Tell me that I am the only one in your heart!" Axel snarled at her and shook her hand just a little.

Tears welled in Annabelle's eyes. "Yes—yes, of course, you are the only one in my heart, Axel. I've changed my mind. I promise you that I have changed my mind!"

Axel held onto Annabelle's wrist for a moment longer before finally letting it go. Annabelle quickly held her hand to her chest and rubbed it against her stomach, but it didn't make the pain go away.

"And the candies. Aren't you thankful I brought them? Aren't you grateful to me?" Axel snapped and shoved the bag once more towards her.

He's mad. He is utterly mad, Annabelle thought. She nodded at once and reached to take one of the sweets. "Thank you, Axel, you look after me so well." She popped it in her mouth and smiled. In truth, it was almost cloyingly sweet after having next to no food for the last couple of days.

The bandit seemed to mollify a little at that and nodded to himself. "I do, don't I? Yes, and once Trace Cassidy and the other little problems are out of the way, there won't be anything to distract you."

Out of the way! Annabelle's expression froze. The Rattler was going after him. He had lied all along.

I have to get out of here. Annabelle knew. And the only way to do that was through the Rattler himself.

"A—Axel?" Annabelle tried to say as sweetly as possible. "I—I know that this was for my own good." She waved her tied hand, which now had a red rash around where the rope had bitten in.

"But do we need it now? Now that we have come to an understanding?" She did her best to look hurt, and it wasn't hard, given her current circumstances.

Axel frowned suspiciously, looking at her wrist and then into her eyes. She was certain that he was going to refuse her, until he nodded, just once, and reached for his belt knife. With a few short swipes, the rope fell apart, and Annabelle felt a relief that almost made her cry for real.

I'm free. That's going to make getting out of here a lot easier.

"I'll get the maid to see to it. I am sorry, my dear, for such extreme measures. But you were addled and not in your right mind. I cannot have my queen as distracted as you were," Axel said, and started to launch into his lecture about how he was going to transform Colorado into a fortress against the rest of the world. It was a speech that Annabelle had heard before, and every time that the Rattler described his perfect city, it got more and more outlandish, and further from reality.

Axel was going to have not one, but three train lines. Axel was going to build a giant gate to the western territories of California. Axel was going to create an inland lake in which they could go boating. The rest of America would treat them like nobility, and so on.

But Annabelle smiled and nodded and said, "Oh goodness" at all the right points until it was time for Axel to go. He stopped his lecture and, as was a ritual now, he brushed the side of her cheek with his hand in what would have been a tender gesture if it had come from literally anyone else.

In the Rattler, it was like a farmer sizing up his livestock.

"Until I see you again, my heart," Axel said.

"I am already missing you!" Annabelle forced herself to say, even though she wanted to gag on the words.

Axel stepped out of the door and barked a command for the older, gray-haired maid to come hurrying in after him. Annabelle waited until the door closed, and the maid was looking at Annabelle's grazed and bruised wrist with a deep frown.

"You got him to take it off? Then you're doing well. Very well." The maid said, She bent down to fish out some liniment from the pockets of her apron, before applying it liberally to Annabelle's wrist.

"It has to be tonight," Annabelle said. "I don't know how much longer I can keep this up. And—and he said that he is going after someone I care for very deeply," Annabelle whispered.

"That will explain why he has all the men around and about," the maid grumbled back. "The whole gang is here. They're going back and forth all the time, but they're not coming back with anything they've stolen. I think they're readying for an attack against the city itself."

Panic struck at Annabelle's heart. Then that meant that the Rattler's plan was almost complete. The bandit might try and kill Trace tonight, even.

I have to warn him!

"Shush, I have a plan—but it's going to be risky," the maid whispered, seeing Annabelle's distress.

"I'm the one who cooks. I'm the one who cleans the Rattler's private chambers. I know where he keeps the laudanum he has been giving you. I'll prepare him a special meal tonight, and make sure he takes it," the maid said. "That will buy you some time—but you won't have long! If I can slip the key to you, then you have a chance."

"Thank you." Annabelle grabbed the woman's old and wrinkled hands and squeezed them.

However scant the opportunity might be to escape right now, or however dangerous—if there was even the most remote chance that she could escape and save Trace's life—then she would take it.

Chapter Twenty-Three

Lamberts' Ranch, Western Colorado Territories, 1866

The old Lamberts' ranch was tucked almost right up against the hills of Calico Pass, where the land started to get wild and scrubby.

"It's past those trees," Trace said, hunkering down on the ground. It was early evening, and the sky was still tinged a burning crimson and purple. Despite the light, it was easy to hide out here, as none of the land had been improved for a generation, and the grasses were tall and thick with small pines and birches springing up everywhere.

"Hm," Sheriff Jackson winced as he shifted his legs and rubbed his hips. The man was already looking old, but Trace had no qualms about his dedication. The man had proven himself to be fearless, despite his quiet demeanor.

"They're already gathering." He nodded at where there was distant movement, and the occasional holler as members of the Rattler's gang arrived and gathered around the gleam of a bonfire.

"They said they weren't going to interfere if we go for the Rattler," Trace murmured—not that he trusted Briggs as far as he could throw him.

"Well, take a look. I can't see him down there." The sheriff offered Trace the spyglass, which he used to scout the area ahead of them.

Suddenly, the surroundings of the Lamberts' old ranch house jumped into stark focus. He couldn't make out much of the house itself, as it was obscured by tree cover, but Trace saw the gleam of some windows, and at least two where lanterns must be hanging inside.

Trace moved the glass to concentrate on the bonfire and saw the movement of men on horseback and on foot. It was hard to keep track of them, as some of the gang had already opened kegs of moonshine and a small party appeared to be taking place—but he guessed there had to be at least fifteen of them.

He saw Briggs, still on his horse and looking nervous. Trace wondered if that meant that Briggs was trying to double-cross him, to lure him out on his own before he caught him.

But Briggs doesn't know that I have the sheriff and his men with me, Trace thought with grim determination.

"I'll move forward to those trees," Trace nodded ahead, "while you bring the posse around the front. Ride in hard, and we should be able to capture most of them."

"It could turn into a pretty fight," the sheriff said.

"It could." Trace nodded. "But we have the upper hand. We'll take them by surprise, and we're about evenly matched."

Actually, their forces only numbered twelve compared to the outlaws' fifteen, *and* Trace had no idea how many were in the house.

But if I can capture Briggs and most of the gang, then the Rattler will know that it's all over for him, Trace nodded to himself.

But the Rattler wasn't there. He was supposed to be there, so Briggs could hand him over.

And there was only one reason why the Rattler wouldn't be there already, wasn't there? Trace grimaced. Briggs clearly hadn't decided to hand him over. This was all a ruse to bring *him,* Trace Cassidy, here. Probably so that the Rattler could kill him.

So there really was only one option left—and that was to take out the gang now.

"You want to wait until it's dark?" The sheriff nodded up to the skies. It wouldn't be long; another hour and full night would be upon them.

"No." Trace shook his head. "We have to act now, in case the Rattler decides to command Briggs and the others to start a raid. I would rather capture them here, like this, than have to chase them down on the open plain."

Jackson nodded and started to get up, but Trace gestured to him.

"And one other thing, Sheriff." Trace remembered the weight of the grenades in his hand, and he remembered the screams in the night. It was eerie how similar this night was to that, with the enemy camp and the fire.

But he was not that man.

"I am going to try and capture and disarm as many as I can. I know that shooting is unavoidable, but I want these men to face justice."

The sheriff blinked in surprise at that. "Why, I am mighty glad to hear you say that, Cassidy. Mighty glad. Nothing would please me more than to haul every man and boy over there up to Denver jail myself!"

At that, the sheriff nodded and started backing through the grasses that led to where the posse and the deputies waited.

"Okay then." Trace started through the grasses towards the trees when he heard a scuffle behind him.

It was Harlan, keeping low as he ran forward, panting for air and with his rifle in his hand.

"Trace!"

"Harlan? What are you doing here? I thought I told you to stay with the others?" Trace hissed back at him. In the 'Briggs' plan, he was supposed to present himself, alone, to the gang in return for the Rattler. As soon as he stepped out with someone else by his side, they would know that something was up.

"I can't let you do it, Trace. I promised Frankie I would be safe, and I promised myself that I would keep *you* safe." Harlan gave him one of his reckless grins. "It seems to me that the safest place for me is right by your side, in all truth."

Trace wanted to shout at him, but they had run out of time. And *darn it,* but Harlan was probably right. It was going to be mayhem when the sheriff arrived with the rest, probably with people running everywhere.

But what Trace *was* annoyed about was that he wanted the freedom to go after the Rattler if he had to. He couldn't have Harlan getting in the way of that.

"Okay, but hang back. Back up the sheriff when he gets here. We're going to scare them first, you got it?" Trace said, for Harlan to nod seriously.

"When I have ever not listened to you, Trace?" he said.

That made Trace smile crookedly. "Plenty of times. Just not tonight, please."

The two men set off at a run, with Trace in front. He zigzagged from one tree to the next, always trying to keep cover between himself and the fire, and pacing his breathing as he went.

The sounds of the gang drew closer and closer with each pounding foot. Trace dreaded the sudden bark of alarm that they had been spotted, but it appeared that the gang was too occupied with their own entertainments to even think about posting a guard.

Or maybe Briggs told them not to, Trace thought as he hunkered down near the end of the trees. He could see the rest of the Lamberts' ranch house now and saw how it must have once been a very grand affair. It was built of actual stone, and must have cost a fortune to transport up here.

But the years had not been kind to the Lambert residence. The walls were dirty and streaked, and moss and ivy clambered erratically where it could. Most of the windows were little more than tacked curtains.

And somewhere in all of that is Annabelle, Trace gritted his teeth. He paused, waiting to see if there was a way that he could get to the house directly—but there wasn't. There was a clear stretch of ground between here and the house, but as soon as he crossed it, the gang would be onto him.

He turned to look back at the outlaws. Several of them were on the floor or on crates around the fire, and appeared to be settling in. Others were on horseback further out and appeared to be attempting to practice standing on their saddles.

And there was no Rattler.

"Where is he?" Trace muttered to himself as Harlan thumped down a few meters away from him.

Trace couldn't see any sign of the bandit king, which meant he had to be in the house. Briggs had double-crossed him. He'd had no intention of handing him over, had he?

Trace looked back at Harlan, who nodded. He was ready.

Before them was the fire, as well as the nearly prone forms of half a dozen outlaws. The memory of that night, so many years ago at the end of the war, returned to him. Now, it repelled him. The thought that he could kill so easily, and without warning.

That is how outlaws fight. Not how men fight.

"Warning shots first, and keep firing. We want to drive them toward the sheriff, not kill them," Trace said. Harlan nodded once again and raised his rifle in the air.

Trace swapped his rifle for his two pistols and carefully raised them to point over the heads of the bandits.

3...2...and—Go!

"Drop yer weapons! You're surrounded!" Trace hollered and fired both pistols in the air as Harlan fired his rifle.

Immediately, the outlaws shrieked in alarm and threw themselves out of the way as Trace and Harlan continued firing. Horses reared and men scrambled for cover, fumbling with their belts.

"We got you! Drop them or die!" Trace shouted again as he fired. At least two of the bandits managed to fire back into the woods, but more than half of them were trying to run toward the far side of the yard—right where Trace wanted them to go.

"Fight back, damn it! Fight!" Trace heard Briggs yell and saw the bandit lieutenant rallying his men as he wheeled his horse around a stationary wagon.

Briggs had at least four men behind the wagon with him that Trace could count. They were hunkering down—and that meant they weren't going to back down. With a snarl of anger, Trace saw that the cover the wagon provided meant that Briggs had a clear line of sight to the trees *and* the end of the yard where the sheriff was due to arrive.

They would be almost impossible to budge. Not without a lot of people dying.

"Cover!" Trace shouted, directing Harlan towards the wagon as he spied a series of crates and barrels a short run from the trees. If he got to the crates, they could corner Briggs at the wagon. Maybe he could even help the sheriff when he turned up.

Trace's eyes flickered to the still, as-yet quiet Lambert house, looming over all of them. *But it would put my back to the windows.*

It was a danger. A very *high* danger—but what could he do? Watch as Briggs and his cronies slaughtered Sheriff Jackson or Frankie's fiancé?

Something his brother had once said to him swam into his mind. One of the last things Wade had said, in fact. "You take your chances in this life." Trace tensed.

Harlan started firing his rifle at the wagon, and Trace saw wood splinters explode from the wheels and wooden side boards. Trace threw himself forward, skidding over the dirt as stray bullets hit the ground around his feet. For a moment, he was flying over the yard, seeing the house to his left, the wagon and the rest of the open yard to his right.

Outlaws were running, mounting their horses. Some were firing wildly into the woods.

The bonfire was in the middle, and nearby were the crates that the outlaws had been sitting on. He jumped, hitting the floor in a roll as he skidded to the crates. Wood burst from their outer edge as Trace tried to make himself as low as possible.

"Varmints! Yer under arrest, the lot of you!"

Sheriff Jackson's voice rose over the tumult, followed by the wild thunder of hooves as the rest of the posse arrived at the mouth of the yard. The deputies and the good men of Colorado City had started by firing into the air—but the already mounted outlaws took the opportunity to gallop towards them.

Gunfire crackled through the air. Trace squirmed his head just in time to see the posse lose its first man. Heathrow Jenkins, the muscled blacksmith of the city, grunted as he was shot from his horse.

No!

Trace hadn't wanted this evening to end in a slaughter. He didn't want this fight to be like the war. He realized now what a fool he had been. Briggs was a wild animal—a man who lived by the gun. He was never going to back down easily, even with half of his men fleeing.

It was chaos at the front of the yard as half of the bandits galloped around and through the sheriff's posse. Trace saw Cephas launching himself clear from his horse to catch one of the outlaws in a bear hug and slam him to the ground.

Instantly, Trace's worst fears were being turned into reality right before his eyes. Sheriff Jackson was trying to marshal his force to arrest as many as possible, but they were being fired on by Briggs and his hardcore outlaws behind the wagon. Some of the bandits broke free and were galloping for the open plains, and some of the posse were giving chase.

In short, it was going to be a bloodbath unless they ended it *now.*

"Wagon!" Trace yelled, hoping that Harlan heard him. He still had his two pistols in hand, so he raised one and started firing wildly at the wagon in order to keep Briggs occupied.

It worked. As his first pistol ran out of bullets, he pointed his second at the wagon—but underneath it, between the wheels—and fired.

"Urk!"

Trace didn't know who he'd hit, but he knew that a wound would make them think twice. It might even make them retreat-

"Hyagh!"

An explosion of dirt covered him as one of the bandits on horseback vaulted clear over Trace's position. Trace saw a flash of horse's hooves and felt a wash of air hit his face.

"Boss! *Boss!*" The bandit was shouting, landing on the other side and wheeling his horse back around towards Trace.

Darn it! Trace had only one pistol with bullets in it. He had no idea if it was going to be enough, or how many bullets he had left. He fired up at the bandit rearing his steed over him—and then had no choice but to roll out of the way.

Trace was in the open. He sprang up from the dirt, and saw acres of blank windows in front of him, at any one of which there could be a gunman.

The hooves of the bandit's horse slammed into the dirt where Trace had been lying; he jumped towards the man, diving out of the way so that he would have to turn his horse around yet again...

A hail of bullets hit the floor as Briggs opened fire. Trace only just managed to jump behind the bandit and reached up to pull him from his horse before the bandit suddenly jerked. Briggs—or one of his own bandits—had accidentally shot him in the side!

Trace saw blood dribble from the side of the man's face before he suddenly fell forward as the horse sprang aside in panic. Thinking quickly, Trace jumped in the same direction the horse was, knowing that if he didn't, he would be left standing in the open, right in the line of fire.

Time seemed to slow. Trace ran, and for a wild moment, he had no idea *where* he was running—just away from the open.

But then, right in front of him was the bonfire—and on the other side of it sat the wagon.

Now was his chance. Trace extended one foot and then the other, his boots pounding on the ground as he saw the fire grow suddenly large in his view, and then...he jumped.

Trace felt heat wrap its hungry embrace around his legs, and then he was sailing through the fire, hitting the ground on the other side as figures burst out from around the wagon towards him.

He pulled the trigger, hip-shooting one of the bandits down. The other shot at him, but it was wild, and Trace skidded to one side—and kicked the fire in a spray of sparks and burning wood.

"Aaargh!"

The bandit stopped in his tracks as burning embers scattered over his face and hands. Trace pulled his trigger to feel the familiar click. He was out of bullets in both guns. He snarled in frustration and instead brought the butt of his pistol down against the man's temples.

"Cassidy!" A shout rose over the scene as the battle raged around him.

Briggs was defiant, standing atop the wagon and snarling at him, with a pistol in his hand.

Trace dove for the wounded bandit's dropped gun as Briggs fired. He felt a searing pain strike his face, and he spun, hitting the side of the wagon...but with the stolen gun in his hand.

"You double-crossed me! You think I let anyone get away with that?" Briggs yelled, firing at the wooden boards as Trace ducked and scrambled under the wagon itself.

Trace heard the thump of Briggs' feet on the boards above him as the bandit dodged and jumped on the wagon bed. "Maybe I should just *let* the Rattler have you!" Briggs screeched.

There was a boom, and wood splintered from the bottom of the wagon bed as Briggs fired almost straight down. Trace hissed, scrabbling to one side—just before there was another boom, and another hole burst through the wooden boards on the other side of Trace.

Am I trapped? Trace froze. Perhaps Briggs was firing blindly. Or perhaps he was guessing where he was.

"Have I killed you yet, you wretch? You still down there, huh, Cassidy?"

Another hole burst through the boards, and this time it was right between Trace's spreadeagled legs.

Trace could still hear shouts and the screams of braying horses outside as the battle continued, but it sounded like it had moved off from the main yard. All that was left here were Briggs and Trace.

He had to get out of here, but Trace knew that any movement might give his position away to the man hunting him just a few inches above. He could fire his own gun up, but Trace didn't know how many bullets it had left in it, and the chances of killing the unseen man or even hitting him were slim.

"You should have died in that war, Cassidy. That's what soldiers do. They die. They're not supposed to come back!" Briggs crowed, and the boards thumped once again as Trace gathered he was lining up for another good shot.

The edge of the wagon was only a short way away. He could be out of here in one roll if he had to...

"Hey!"

Suddenly, Harlan's voice burst across the yard, and it was followed by a scrape of boots on the boards above him. Trace rolled, grabbing the edge of the wagon as he hauled himself up.

He heard Briggs' gunshot as he threw himself up the far side of the wagon—and rose just in time to see Harlan hitting the floor by the trees.

"No!"

Trace yelled. Images of his brother, Wade, falling right next to him rose in his eyes.

Briggs was standing by the back board, his gun still smoking from having shot Harlan. The bandit spun around, his gun leveling against Trace...

Trace pulled his own trigger instinctively. The bullet tore through Briggs' chest and threw him from the wagon bed to hit the ground with a heavy thump.

"Harlan! *Harlan!*" Trace kept his pistol covering the dead brigand as he jogged back towards the trees—just as Harlan groaned and pushed himself upright.

"I'm fine, Trace. I think he just missed me." Harlan was pulling at his jacket, where a visible tear ran along where his ribs would be. The younger man looked up and grimaced.

"Although I don't know if I can say the same thing for you," Harlan said.

Huh?

It was then that Trace felt the warmth that had been dribbling down the side of his face. Reaching up, he suddenly felt an explosion of pain in his ear.

"Ach! He must have winged me, too."

"An inch to the left and he would have taken out your eye." Harlan's voice was almost faint with shock.

But Trace had no time for shock. The fight was still raging between the sheriff's posse and the bandits, further out over the scrubby meadow.

And Annabelle was still in the house somewhere.

"Stay low. Try to pick off what bandits you can." Trace told Harlan at once, before he turned back to fix his gaze on the house.

I'm coming, Annabelle, he promised, and broke into a loping run.

Chapter Twenty-Four

Lamberts' Ranch, Western Colorado Territories, 1866

The front door was standing empty and unguarded as Trace ran up to the stone porch and forced himself to breathe.

He quickly jammed spare bullets and powder from his ammo belt into his stolen gun—glad that at least he and the bandit had the same make of pistol, a Colt .45 Dragoon revolver.

Heaven save her. Give me the strength to get Annabelle back safely. Trace prayed quickly, before loping into the blank space, and seeing nothing but darkness for a moment.

His eyes adjusted, and he saw the large entry foyer, with doors on either side of him and a staircase leading up to a gallery section above. The foyer might once have been a grand affair, with checkered tiles on the floor and proper wood-paneled walls, but years of neglect had mired and cracked the tiles, and patches of dark mold grew on the wood.

So this is your kingdom, is it, Rattler? Trace sneered. He kept his gun up at the gallery above as he edged towards the first door—just before he heard a gasp from above him.

"Trace!"

He would know that voice anywhere. *Annabelle!* Trace spun around to see that she was above him on the gallery, emerging from a room and looking down at him with her face half full of hope—half full of fear. She looked pale, and her dress was the same one that she had been wearing days ago, looking disheveled and grubby.

"He's asleep—we have to get her and go!" Annabelle whispered fiercely.

What? Trace didn't understand what she was trying to tell him, but whatever it was, he didn't care. He started towards the stairs as she ran down the gallery towards him.

"Hgnurgh!"

With an almighty crash, the next door on the upstairs gallery between Annabelle and the stairs flung itself open, and the form of the Rattler himself careened out, his gun blazing.

It was him. Trace snarled. It was really him, the same man who had killed his parents. He had the same wild and dark hair, now shot through with gray. He had the same barrel chest, which wore a fine waistcoat and high breeches.

And he had on a pair of red leather gloves, clearly replacements for the ones he had lost.

"Annabelle—down!" Trace shouted, diving forwards as bullets hit the banisters and the stairs around him. He didn't want to fire a shot back, not with Annabelle so close.

Trace hit the landing on his side, rolling and jumping to his feet as Annabelle leapt to his level.

He caught her with one hand and fired two sharp return shots back at the Rattler to make him dive back into the room he had just come out of. Trace knew that the bandit king wasn't wounded; he was just diving for cover.

"Trace—*go!* RUN!" Annabelle gasped.

There was another roar from the room, and a crash as Trace grabbed Annabelle's hand and jumped down the stairs.

I have to get her safe. She has to be safe!

They were almost at the bottom when the screaming started above them—and the bullets started flying once more.

"ANNABELLE!"

Trace pulled Annabelle to one side as a bullet split the last stair tread. Another struck one of the floor tiles of the lobby, shattering it—and then a third hit the door frame.

"The dining room!" Trace knew at once that they would get shot in the back if they made a dash for the door. He dove left instead, flinging them both through the dining room door to land on the floor, with Annabelle on top of him.

"Oof!"

"I'm sorry, did I hurt you?" Annabelle was the first to her feet and was already grabbing Trace's hand when they heard the sound of thumping feet charging down the stairs. The Rattler was after them, and he was charging like a bull.

Trace fired a shot at the open doorway into the lobby—but it didn't even seem to slow the Rattler down.

"I'm coming for you, Annabelle! I won't let this *mutt* have you!"

Trace and Annabelle ran down the length of the dining room, past a long oval table where apparently the Rattler must have held court, as there were spilled flagons and glasses everywhere, along with stacks of plates with pipe ashes or cigars stubbed out on top of them.

"There must be a kitchen with a back door out of here!" Trace gasped, skidding through the open door at the back to see that they were in some kind of servants' hallway.

"Which way?" Trace hissed.

"I don't know! I was drugged!" Annabelle whispered.

What? The revelation went into Trace's mind and made him furious... But now was not the time for that. Now was the time to survive.

The hallway ran right and left on either side of them, and, figuring that wherever they went it had to at least to a window they could break, Trace chose left.

The hallway was narrow, and he did his best to try and minimize his footprints, but their breathing alone would surely tell the Rattler where they were. Trace wanted to turn and face him...but right now, all that he wanted was to get Annabelle to safety.

I'll get her through a window and then turn back, he decided. In fact, that would be a whole lot better because then that would just be himself and the Rattler in this big old house, wouldn't it?

The corridor went past more doors that seemed to lead deeper into the house. Trace got a sense that would lead them back to where the Rattler was.

Hang on. Where IS the Rattler? Trace paused, doing his best to quieten his breathing.

"What is it?" Annabelle skidded to a halt beside him.

Trace shook his head. "Listen." He held up a finger, pointing to nothing but the air itself.

There was nothing. No ticks, no clicks, and no sound of footsteps charging after them. Of course, Trace knew that could mean that it could be that the walls were just exceptionally thick in the Lamberts' maisonette. But to Trace, it seemed as though the Rattler had given up searching for them.

"But why would he do that?" Trace murmured. "Why wouldn't he be chasing us?" He looked up to see Annabelle regarding him with wide eyes. She had deep circles under her eyes, where it looked like she either hadn't slept or had hardly eaten anything in a week.

"He knows this place well, doesn't he?" Trace whispered. "So he must know all the routes out of this place. It's my betting that as soon as we went down the servants' hall—he moved to cut us off."

"Okay." Annabelle nodded. "So. What do we do? Go back?"

Trace thought about it, and in truth, it sounded like one of the best options. If the Rattler was trying to outsmart them, then they could surely do the same right back to him.

"He appeared mostly drunk anyway," Trace admitted to himself.

"Drugged. We managed to get some of the drugs into his food. It was all a part of our plan to escape." Annabelle whispered.

Ours? Trace looked at her quizzically. He still couldn't get over the fact that it was her, and she was actually, really here. Even in her current condition, with her hair knotted and tangled and her skin pale, there was still more vitality in her than Trace had seen in anyone.

"Someone helped me. The servant maid here. I can't—we have to help her escape too!" Annabelle reached for his hand and clasped it. Trace felt the warmth of her skin like a blessing.

Trace stopped, still listening intently for any signs of pursuit. There were none. He wanted nothing more than to get Annabelle out of there. But he saw the way she furrowed her brow and bit her lower lip in determination.

Annabelle Flint was a determined woman. There was nothing that he would be able to do about it if she decided to stay.

"Okay. Do you know where she is?" Trace whispered.

"I was kept in a locked room, but I think she must have been staying somewhere in the upstairs bedrooms." A look of anguish crossed Annabelle's face. "Oh, Trace—I can't leave this place until I know she is free. If anything were to happen to her..."

"I get it," Trace nodded. He knew that kind of loyalty. He had felt that same fierce love for his brothers during the war. It was the invisible bond that wove between them.

What a woman, Trace took a breath. Annabelle was fierce and brave and loyal. As much, if not more, than any soldier he had fought alongside.

"Okay. Try to stay behind me. And as soon as we see the Rattler, I want you to run, okay?" Trace said, and Annabelle nodded.

Trace made to turn around, back the way they had come, but before he could, he felt Annabelle's hand squeeze his own.

"And Trace...?" Her breath was the slightest, breathy murmur.

"Yes?" He turned to her quickly. Was she hurt, and she hadn't told him? Was she scared?

Her eyes were large and dark as they sought his own. "I missed you. I'm glad I found you again," she whispered.

Trace felt his heart swell. But it wasn't with fear—it was with love.

"I wouldn't be anywhere else," he promised.

Trace led her back up the corridor, pausing at each door until he was sure he could hear nothing inside, before returning to the dining room. It was quiet in there, with the still air only occasionally broken by the muted, distant crack of a gunshot outside the house.

The battle had moved off, Trace realized. And it sounded like it was quieting down. He prayed that the sheriff had won.

"Be careful." Trace whispered, stepping around the smashed glass and the turned-over chairs. Drabs of wasted food had been spilled over the table—but there was no Rattler.

"Where did he go!" Annabelle whispered. "Do you think he went outside? Maybe he ran?"

"No." Trace shook his head. He knew who the Rattler was. He knew *what* the Rattler was, and seeing him earlier after not seeing him for years only confirmed it.

The Rattler was a monster who had lain in wait for the best part of ten years, all in order to get what he wanted. He wasn't going to stop.

Which is why I have to stop him, Trace glowered.

"He's waiting for us." Trace muttered. "This is what he does. He sneaks, waits until he has the upper hand—and then strikes. He's a snake."

"A *mad* snake," Annabelle said. He felt her hand settle on his shoulder. Although she was probably comforting herself, Trace felt a surge of confidence.

Trace stepped out of the dining room and back into the hallway, his gun sweeping the open front door and the upstairs gallery. Still nothing, and no creak of floorboards or gasps of breath.

Come out, come out and face me! Trace gritted his teeth in a silent snarl.

"Upstairs. The maid's room is one of those." Annabelle murmured in his ear. Trace nodded and started forward, one careful step at a time.

Trace swept the room opposite—that might have been some kind of study, only all it contained now were open crates of moonshine and stacks of riding equipment. He turned back...

He heard a slight gasp from above them, a noise that was almost too low to hear.

"He's got her!" Annabelle immediately ran for the stairs, her face looking urgent.

"*Wait!*" Trace hissed, running after her.

Annabelle got to the top landing just before he did, and turned to the gallery level. He could tell she wasn't thinking about anything other than saving her friend.

"*Annabelle!*" Trace ran after her, reaching the landing a few steps behind—just in time to see a dark shape burst from one of the open doors, and the Rattler catching Annabelle by the dark hair that streamed from her bun.

No!

"What did you do, girly? What did you *do*?" The Rattler roared, dragging Annabelle back towards him. His words were slurring, and he wobbled on his feet as he grabbed Annabelle close to him, with his own pistol, shoving it towards her belly.

"Stop!" Trace yelled at once. He pointed his gun directly at the Rattler's head, but Annabelle was struggling wildly, and he couldn't shoot.

"It's over, Rattler. Unhand her *now,* and I'll let you live," Trace demanded.

But the Rattler ignored him. He appeared to only have eyes for Annabelle, as he shoved the pistol hard into her belly.

"Why did you do this to me, Anna? What have I ever done to you? To think that I was going to give you everything. *Everything!"* The man wailed, his voice breaking.

He was unhinged, Trace could see that. The man was obsessed with Annabelle, and she had just done the worst thing she could to a man like him—by choosing Trace Cassidy instead.

"Let go of me! I hate you! I hate everything about you!" Annabelle screamed.

"You're lying. *He* has gotten into your mind. He's poisoned you. I was going to make you a queen, Anna." The Rattler growled.

Annabelle was still struggling, and the Rattler was still shoving and dragging her in front of him, so that Trace couldn't get a clear shot. He rose from the floor, blocking the stairs.

"I would rather be dead than be with you!" Anna shouted, before suddenly gasping in pain.

The Rattler increased his stranglehold about her neck, and it was so tight that Trace saw her face start to blush. The Rattler hissed into her ear, his voice low and terrible.

"Maybe it will come to that yet, my sweet. Maybe it will. If I cannot have you—then no one should!"

"Drop it, Rattler!" Trace shouted. "It's over. Your gang is gone. Briggs is dead. Your only hope now is letting Annabelle go, and maybe I'll spare your life." Trace tried to track her movements, but the Rattler was keeping her between them. Finally, he flickered a glance towards Trace himself.

"This is all your fault, you know," the Rattler sneered at him. "You are going to lose the woman you pretend to love, and it will be your fault. Just like you lost your parents."

"Shut up." Trace demanded. He felt ice-cold rage running through him.

The Rattler pushed Annabelle forward, towards the landing. "You are going to go back down those stairs, and you are going to drop your gun, Trace Cassidy. You are going to do exactly what I tell you because you are no hero. You are still just a little boy who cannot even save his parents!"

Trace's jaw clenched at that. So the Rattler remembered him, did he? Somehow, that made this worse. It made it personal.

"I know that you are going to obey my orders, Trace Cassidy." The Rattler took another step, shoving Annabelle towards the landing, which Trace currently blocked.

"And you know why I know? Because you're not going to take that shot. Because you know that you are a bad shot, really. If you were any good, you would have shot me all those years ago, wouldn't you? But you didn't. You missed." The Rattler snarled.

Memories of that long-ago night flooded into Trace's mind. He remembered the heaviness of his father's gun in his hands. He remembered how all time had appeared to slow to that one, tiny moment as he fired.

"I remember hitting you, actually," Trace growled back. He had wounded the Rattler, hadn't he? He remembered the man lurching and grunting in pain.

217

If I could do that as a teenager—what do you think I can do now? Trace thought.

This would-be king of Colorado did not know what Trace had done since then. The Rattler could not know that he had spent years honing his craft as a scout.

Trace had learned his early lesson well.

"Drop the gun or I shoot her!" the Rattler bawled.

Trace's eyes flickered to Annabelle's. The Rattler had her on a grip around the upper shoulders and neck, but Annabelle had her arms around his forearm. He saw her firm, glaring eyes staring back at him—and how she nodded her head, just slightly.

She trusted him. She trusted that he would save her.

Trace nodded—and in that instant, Annabelle threw her whole body to one side, ducking her head with enough force to catch the Rattler off guard for just a fraction of a moment.

Trace pulled the trigger.

The boom was deafening in the wide hall, and gun smoke blew in front of his vision—but when it cleared, he saw that Annabelle was leaning against the wall, and the Rattler was on the floor, with gun smoke rising from him.

It had been a perfect shot. The Rattler was dead.

"Oh, Trace!" Annabelle ran to him then, and Trace found himself folding his arms around her in a way that felt as natural as breathing in and out. She hugged him fiercely, and he held her as her body quivered against his.

And when she lifted her head to his, he kissed her long and deep.

Chapter Twenty-Five

Lamberts' Ranch, Western Colorado Territories, 1866

"I still can't believe it," Annabelle murmured as she walked out of the house and, for the first time in what felt like years— she breathed a sigh of relief. The air smelled of wood smoke and gun smoke, but underneath it, she could smell good, clean, honest Colorado air, and it was blissful.

The scene in front of the ranch looked like a battle had taken place, with a wagon and a bonfire to one side, but also a whole mess of churned-up ground.

And bodies. Annabelle looked away in shock, and at once she felt Trace's hand squeeze hers more strongly, and lead her away from the sight of death towards the side of the house.

"I'm sorry. I didn't think." Trace murmured. "We need to keep you safe."

"I think you've already done that." Annabelle said, although she was grateful to not have to see the bodies. "Is it over? The shoot-out, I mean?"

Trace paused, lifting his head, and Annabelle was amazed she hadn't noticed how chiseled his jawline looked before.

I had been searching for the boy when the man returned from the war, Annabelle realized. She suddenly stopped to see Trace Cassidy differently for the first time. He was no longer the leggy, athletic youth that she remembered from her childhood—the youth that had once been carefree and always adventurous, and who had become quiet and serious after the Rattler took his parents away.

This Trace Cassidy was altogether different. He was broader in the shoulders and with a man's muscle on his frame. Stubble washed over the lower half of his face—and his eyes!

His eyes were clear and blue just as they always were, but Annabelle didn't remember them being so piercing, or containing such depths.

I love this man, don't I? she admitted to herself.

"I think the shooting has stopped," Trace said. He was holding something up to his face. A spyglass.

"Harlan's all right. So is Sheriff Jackson, Cephas... Yes. They did it. They've completely crushed the gang and captured over half of them!" Trace said excitedly, turning back to smile at her. He looked tired, but happy.

Annabelle felt the warmth of his hand in her own, and wondered why she had never noticed his quiet strength before. Or the way he tried so hard.

A look of worry crossed his face then. "Are you in pain? Did he...?" Trace's voice lowered to a bare whisper as he dared not say any more, but Annabelle shook her head at once.

"He didn't lay a finger on me. None of them did."

A look of relief crossed Trace's face then. "I'm glad he didn't hurt you. I couldn't bear it, knowing that he had you here and..."

Annabelle shook her head at the unpleasant memory. If she never thought about those dark days ever again, then she would be more than happy. She gestured up at the blood that had dried to a blackened sleet all over his cheek, and the ruined, torn-open ear lobe that Trace now sported.

"Well. I think that I should be asking you the same questions. You look a state, Trace." She reached up tenderly, but at the merest brush of her fingers, Trace winced.

"Oh, I'm sorry. There's water in the house. And there's laudanum. I know that there's that." Annabelle pulled a face.

She took a breath and realized that she was scared of telling Trace exactly what had happened. She was scared of ever being that vulnerable to anyone.

But this was the man who had risked his life to come to you. He risked everything, Annabelle reminded herself.

And—she loved him. She felt safe standing here, holding his hand.

"He drugged me." Annabelle admitted. "I think a part of him knew that he couldn't keep me there any other way. He added laudanum to my food, and I never even knew what time it was or how many days had passed."

"That's awful. The man was a monster." Trace gritted his teeth. He looked away, and Annabelle saw that there was a great shame in him.

"What, Trace? What is it? He's gone. The Rattler is gone now." She gave his hand a little squeeze.

"I wish I had brought him to justice. I wish he would have to stand before a court of his peers and explain his actions—and receive his punishment. It almost seems like he got the easy way out." Trace said.

"He's never going to hurt anyone ever again." Annabelle said firmly. "That is all that I care about. Just so long as I can live the rest of my life in peace, knowing that the Rattler isn't out there somewhere, or at risk of escaping—then yes, I can be happy." She sighed and knew what she had said was true. This

221

part of her life was finally over. This part of *both* of their lives was finally over.

"*You're* free too, Trace," she whispered to him, and reached up very slowly to put a hand on his cheek. She was careful not to touch his wounded ear, and felt the crackle of dried blood against his stubble.

"Nothing is going to bring back who he took," Trace admitted.

"No." Annabelle said solemnly. She thought about her parents, and her family, and she thought about Trace's parents, who had fallen due to the Rattler.

"But we get to make something new now. Even with those losses—with those memories—we get to build something that doesn't have the Rattler's shadow over it," she said, and meant every word of it.

He looked into her eyes then, and Annabelle felt her heart melt. She was meant to be with this man. She was destined to be with this man, she knew.

"Annabelle," Trace said in a deep and husky voice.

"*Mistress!*"

They were suddenly interrupted by the sound of a shout, as the maid stumbled out of the house behind them, holding a wooden broom handle in her hand and looking around her warily. Trace spun around at once, his hand automatically going for the gun in his belt.

"It's alright!" Annabelle said hurriedly. "This is my friend. She saved me."

"Oh!" Trace, once relaxed, broke contact with Annabelle as he rushed forward to offer the older woman his arm.

"Oh, I'm not that old yet, young man," the maid said. She looked tired, but she was beaming. She winked at Annabelle.

"This is him, is it? Your sweetheart?" the maid said.

"Uh..." Annabelle looked at Trace to see him regarding her with a slightly raised eyebrow. Is this what they were to each other now? What if that kiss had just been in the passion of the moment? What if Trace went back to his surly, silent ways, just as he had been before the war?

What right did she even have to say how their lives were going to be now?

"Yes." Trace laughed, reaching out to grab her hand and hold it up for a moment. "A thousand times, yes."

Annabelle laughed. *I never knew you had the passion in you, Trace Cassidy!*

Annabelle could feel herself blushing. She took hold of the maid's other arm. "She was one of the Lamberts when the Rattler took over, and he kept her as a slave as I am sure he was going to do to me. She drugged the Rattler so that I could escape."

Trace appeared delighted. "Then I thank you, Madame Lamberts, from the bottom of my heart. I swear that you shall have a job and a home with us, from this day forth."

The older maid blinked at that, but she looked overjoyed. Madame Lamberts took a deep breath and sighed, and it seemed to Annabelle that years of stress fell from her shoulders.

"I'm going to need help at the ranch," Annabelle said a little awkwardly. She was aware of Trace's every movement and how his body felt, so close to her.

Because I guess this is it now, isn't it? Annabelle thought. Now that the Rattler was gone, she would go back to her old life. While a part of her felt happy about that—she had to admit to feeling sad, too.

What was going on with that!?

She had grown close to the Cassidys these last few months. They were the only family she had left.

And this is the man I love.

She looked up to find that Trace had stepped away from Madame Lamberts, but he still held her hand. He was looking at her with an intensity that made her knees feel weak.

"Do you want to live at your family ranch, Annabelle?" His voice was low and gravelly, as a wolf might talk, or a bear.

"Well, yes, of course." She stammered just slightly. She felt breathy, but not scared at all.

Trace looked shy for a fraction of a second. "Do you want to stay there alone, I guess I mean."

What? Annabelle's eyes flickered to Madame Lamberts, hovering behind Trace and looking as though she was about to burst out laughing, although Annabelle had no idea why.

"Well, I guess I wouldn't be, not really…"

"What I mean is, Annabelle…" Trace cleared his throat and suddenly dropped down to one knee.

Oh!

"Annabelle Flint, would you do me the honor of marrying me?" Trace asked.

Annabelle couldn't believe what she was hearing. Trace Cassidy loved her. He felt the same as she felt about him. How long for? And why hadn't he said anything sooner!

Heat rushed to her cheeks; of course, she was going to say yes. In that moment, she knew that she was always going to say yes to Trace Cassidy from the time that they first knew each other.

"I will, Trace," Annabelle laughed. Trace's face lifted into a beaming smile—until Annabelle carried on.

"But you have to ask me again somewhere nice. Not right outside the place where I was kept—or next door to a battlefield!" she laughed.

Trace's face fell suddenly, looking alarmed. "Of course! Of course, why didn't I think of that!" He flustered, but Annabelle was laughing all the way through.

"It's alright, Trace, you can get up off the floor. I said yes, didn't I?" She laughed.

Trace did get up from the floor, just as Sheriff Jackson and Harlan rode up.

"Annabelle!" Harlan called out, then his face creased in confusion when he saw the pair of them giggling. "What's so funny?"

"Nothing." Annabelle shook her head. "Nothing at all. I am just very, very glad to be back. And with all of you."

She looked at Trace and felt his strong hand twist into hers.

Chapter Twenty-Six

Cassidy Ranch, 1867

I do. Trace couldn't help but grin to himself as the wagon jostled and trembled underneath him. He looked down at his bare hands holding the reins and at the plain gold band that now sat on his wedding finger.

"I did. I always did," he murmured, feeling his jaw ache with the amount of grinning he was doing.

How was this his life? How had it gone from such misery to such glory?

Because of Annabelle, that's why. He turned his head, looking past the faces of Cephas and Sawyer behind him on the wagon, along with the mounds of canvas and the boxes of party preparations. His eyes found Annabelle, riding alongside Frankie and Harlan, and throwing her head back in laughter.

She looked glorious, of course, with her long black hair brushed until it shone in the Colorado sun. She still wore her plain white blouse, and there was a bouquet of prairie flowers pinned to her shoulder strap. But she had replaced her long white skirts with more sensible trews for the ride home, as well as long leather riding boots.

Trace grinned. Apparently, that blouse and skirt had caused Frankie and Madame Lamberts no end of trouble in designing and making, as Annabelle had insisted that she be able to change so that she could "ride decently, without any bother and trouble!"

He liked that about Annabelle. She could look as rare and as graceful as a prairie rose, but she would also roll up her sleeves and stick on riding chaps just to get a job done. A sense of warm promise filled Trace's heart. With a wife like that, anything was possible. He swore he could feel his life opening up ahead of him—and the horizon was endless.

"Stop gawking, son!" Old Mr. Sawyer suddenly shouted, pointing at the track ahead. Trace turned quickly around to see that he was in imminent danger of driving them straight into a pothole as deep as he was wide.

Trace clicked and pulled the reins sharply, for Bella and the other horse to skip a little, and pull the wagon clear of danger.

"Can't blame the man." Cephas laughed loudly. "He has just got married, hasn't he? I'm surprised he agreed to drive the wagon at all. If it were me, I'd hightail it out of here!"

Sawyer and Cephas laughed, and even Trace shared a grin. In truth, there was nothing that he wanted better to do than to get out of there, with Annabelle at his side.

But Annabelle's ranch was still a whole lot less than functional after the fire, and it would take months to rebuild the damage that the Rattler's gang had done. Trace felt a shadow of frustration at that.

But at least he's gone. They're all gone now.

Sheriff Jackson, along with Cephas and Harlan, had chased down and rounded up the last of Brigg's gang, with only two men managing to escape onto the prairies, heading north. For the next couple of weeks after that, Trace and Sheriff Jackson had ridden up to Denver twice to try and convince the Denver sheriff to take action. Jackson had received a telegram just yesterday morning to say that the Denver sheriff and his deputies had finally caught the two remaining men of the Rattlers gang, attempting to sneak out of town.

It was done. The entire gang—both gangs, if you counted Clay Slade as well—were broken. And the Rattler was gone.

The timing couldn't be better for Trace. It felt like a weight he hadn't even known he was carrying had finally lifted from his shoulders. To think that he had spent years being haunted by those men, and had just accepted that they were always going to be out there somewhere!

Trace lifted his head, letting Annabelle's laughter bring a smile to his lips and the Colorado sun warm his face. He felt like a changed man.

But not a new man, Trace blinked, and looked back at the road ahead. He was still Trace Cassidy. He could still feel that place inside of him forged by war, and born from a long-ago night, when he had held a revolver too heavy and his breath was filled with smoke.

Instead, he felt like he could carry all the parts of himself easily. He felt bigger than the wolfish soldier or the angry child. He was all of them and so, so much more.

"I'm a husband now." Trace murmured to himself, looking up as there was a clatter of hooves, and Annabelle rode up to his wagon, winking at him as she settled in beside him.

"The rest of the folks are on their way, husband," she said, grinning. He could see that she was just as happy as he was.

"Then we'd better hurry." Trace laughed, nodding to where the Cassidy ranch houses rose in the distance.

In the near paddock, they had staked out a large marquee, and the form of Madame Lamberts—who hadn't been at this morning's wedding, so she could continue preparing for the celebration afterwards—was moving back and forth from the tent to the house.

"She's done a beautiful job." Annabelle sighed. Madame Lamberts had strung more bouquets of flowers along the front of the marquee, as well as laying them out in a wide trail towards the marquee itself.

Bees hummed over the meadows, and the sky had just the right amount of scudding clouds and light wind.

"It's going to be a fine night for dancing." Annabelle shot him another wink.

Trace grinned. "I haven't been known to kick my legs for a while..." he said.

"Oh, I'm sure you'll do just fine, old man." Annabelle laughed.

Old man? Trace chuckled at that. He was only a few years older than her. He would show her a thing or two about dancing!

They arrived with the bluster of smiles, more congratulations, and good humor from everyone. Madame Lamberts brought out some cold meats and a little wine for them to break their fast, and before long, everyone got to work on the final preparations.

Trace and Harlan chopped and carried wood for the bonfire. Annabelle and Frankie got the last of the food ready. Cephas and Sawyer worked on the yard and the tent, just as the first of their wedding guests started to arrive.

Everyone who was anyone appeared to want to be at the Cassidy wedding. First and foremost was Sheriff Jackson, his wife Eda, and even their mature son William had come all the way from Chicago, where he was a deputy over there.

The Widow Moats arrived with a small delegation of fellow shopkeepers and store holders, as did Mr. Haversham the

ZACHARY MCCRAE

tailor, bringing with him his wife and brood of five children, each exquisitely dressed in the latest fashions.

Trace was much relieved with the gaggle of fiddlers and musicians, who arrived sporting a variety of stringed instruments and at least one flute. They wasted no time in joyously starting a beat on their drums, playing non-stop for the next few hours, and long into the evening.

A parade of food was brought to the tables not just by Frankie and Madame Lamberts, but also many of the wives of Colorado City, and barrels of beer had been donated by some of the local saloons.

By the time that the sun was starting to burn the western horizon, the drink had brought a rosy flush to people's cheeks, and a constant round of dancing was ongoing in the main yard, with different groups forming circles and whirl-y-gigs.

Trace collapsed after dancing down one line, begging off another round as he raised his head to look for his good lady wife. In truth, they had managed to only catch a little bit of time with each other during the long day, as they were constantly called to this or that person's attention.

"Howdy, brother." Frankie appeared, thumping her shoulder against his on the other side of the post of the tent.

"You and Harlan having fun, sister?" Trace smiled at her.

Frankie was flushed too, although he didn't remember seeing her drinking at all. Her eyes were alive and bright as she watched the festivities around them.

"Pa and Ma would have loved this," Frankie said.

Trace winced a little, but smiled all the same. "Pa would have thrown a fit. He would have hated the upset!"

"Ha!" Frankie laughed, dabbing at her eyes. "You're probably right. But Wade would have enjoyed it."

"He would," Trace admitted. He cast a look up at the heavens, where the stars were just starting to come out. "Who knows, maybe he *is* enjoying this somehow, from up there."

"Telling us to get back to the dancing, probably." Frankie laughed. Then she cleared her throat. "Actually, Trace? I have something to tell you."

"Hm?" Trace had turned his eyes to where Cephas was trying to lead Annabelle through a complicated two-step, and she was laughing, holding her retrieved long skirts up as she showed she was more than a match for any dancer here.

"It's about me and Harlan," Frankie said. "We're going to need to build some more space onto the ranch."

"You need more space? Well, me and Annabelle will be out of here in a month or so," Trace said distractedly. He couldn't take his eyes off of Annabelle as she stopped dancing, and then slowly cut a path towards him through the crowd.

"No, I don't think you understand, Trace. Me and Harlan *need some more space,*" Frankie said once again, more heavily.

Is she trying to get rid of us? Trace thought, starting to grin as he flashed a look at his sister, with her hands crossed over her belly.

Over her belly.

Oh. Trace blinked. "Oh."

He looked at her, surprised and elated at the same time. "Do you mean that you are..."

"Sheesh, brother. Yes, I am pregnant. Me and Harlan are expecting a baby." Frankie said the words.

"That's amazing news! Congratulations! I'm going to be an uncle!" Trace whooped, whisking his sister in a hug and whirling her around.

"Easy there, boss." Annabelle laughed from behind him. Trace didn't know how long she had been standing and waiting to talk to them, but from the massive grin on her face, it appeared that she had overheard everything. "You're hurling a pregnant woman around there!"

"Oh, crikey." Trace immediately put the man down, stepping back as if Frankie was made of rare bone china.

Frankie and Angeline looked at each other and then suddenly broke into gales of laughter.

"What?" Trace looked from one to the other, but his sister was shaking her head, patting Annabelle on the shoulder and walking back towards the party, where Harlan was waiting to welcome her.

"Do I have to be careful around her?" Trace asked.

"You have to be careful around me." Annabelle laughed, playfully punching him on the shoulder. He caught her hand and then pulled her into a deep kiss.

They held each other for a long time, and the rest of the world faded away for an eternity. When they finally broke, Trace looked at his wife, the woman he loved. He was surrounded by all the people he loved in the world, and he had Annabelle by his side.

The future felt good.

Epilogue

The Flint-Cassidy Ranch, 1871

"Do you think I could ride him one day?" the little boy said, looking up at his father.

Trace felt Wade's small hand in his own. The skin was so soft and perfect. In time, Trace knew that it would grow callouses. His first-born son would learn to work the animals, and yes, he would learn to ride the horses—even if he couldn't tell that Bella was a girl just yet.

"Her. Bella is a girl's name, silly," Trace laughed. With his free hand, he tousled Wade's hair, that was still a little fine, but the first telltale waves of chestnut gold were starting to appear, just like his father's.

"I want a horse named Champion." Wade stuck out his tongue in thought. "Or Wolf!"

Trace laughed. His son had probably picked up that name because last night Cephas had been over-delivering some presents for Trace's birthday today, and Trace had found the sheriff telling Wade stories about how Trace had been 'the Wolf of the Colorado Mountains' and how he had almost single-handedly driven out two bandit gangs.

Trace thought that his son might be a little too young for such stories yet and didn't quite understand just what outlaws and bandits meant.

Hopefully, he'll never have to know, Trace wished fervently, and promised once again that he would be there just as long as he could to keep Wade from any harm at all.

In truth, Colorado City was getting a lot better. The whole territory was safer now, especially since President Grant had put it in for official statehood under the Union.

They hadn't won that one, not yet—but Trace could tell that it was coming. Colorado was a state in everything but name, anyway. She had cities and she had roads and she had soldiers and sheriffs and schools and courthouses—even the Denver Pacific railroad had recently been completed.

"Are you excited about the new school?" Trace turned to ask his son, as Wade continued to lean on the lowest wooden run of the stalls, looking at their horses speculatively. The stables new, along with the big barn that they had put in a couple years ago. Trace had worked hard to expand Annabelle's family ranch, and they now had a new horse business alongside their main cattle one.

"Yeah. Will there be many children there like me?" Wade looked up at his father.

Trace laughed. "There will be other children your age, certainly. But none of them will be like you. There's only one Wade Flint-Cassidy."

Wade looked suitably pleased at that, grabbed a handful of hay to throw into the air with a loud 'Ha!' Trace seized the opportunity to grab another handful of hay and throw it over the man.

"Ha!" Trace countered, earning a squeal of laughter and another shower of hay.

"*Oi!* Get yerselves in here, you two miscreants!" Annabelle's voice lifted from the main house.

Trace and Wade turned around at once, looking up to see Annabelle standing on the porch, with both fists on her hips.

She was wearing skirts for a change today, which was probably because it was Trace's birthday.

"Oh well, looks like we're in trouble now, son. Don't worry, I'll say it was all your fault," Trace whispered conspiratorially.

"Pa!" Wade wailed, half smiling, half unsure.

But Trace laughed, snatched him up, and hugged him as he strode back out of the open stables to the main house.

Annabelle was grinning as she welcomed them in. Her anger had been a joke, as she playfully swiped at Trace's butt.

"And just because it's your birthday, it doesn't mean that you don't have to get nice and clean for Uncle Harlan and Aunt Frankie!" Annabelle said loudly, before plopping a kiss on Wade's cheek.

Trace winked at his wife, taking in her swelling belly. She was going to be due their second child this autumn, and Trace was hoping for a girl. He would be pleased, however, the child arrived just so long as they were healthy, of course, but he secretly hoped for a girl.

He took his boy into the downstairs washroom and proceeded to get scrubbed up, before changing into some clean clothes. Before they were even done, he heard the clatter of hooves and the shout of happy voices. Harlan and Frankie were here.

"Happy birthday, brother." Frankie greeted him as soon as he walked Wade back out to the yard. Frankie wore her hat and had a package under her arm, but she was watching Jeremiah and Josie, squealing as they ran towards their cousin, Wade. Jeremiah had Wade's wide grin, but Josie had the same wavy gold hair that all the Cassidys had.

"Sis, Harlan." Trace greeted them as Harlan came up to give his hand a shake and pressed a small box into his hand.

"Frankie made you up a new shirt, but I came with the good stuff," he said, tapping the box of limited cigars from the south. Trace grinned, knowing that the younger man was probably looking forward to sharing them tonight after the meal.

Annabelle and Frankie fell in with each other as they always did, swapping small bits of news as they somehow managed to also keep an eye on the rabble of kids that were now whooping and hollering around the yard. Trace and Harlan went inside, where Trace poured his brother-in-law a coffee as he checked on the roast and started dicing the vegetables.

To think that this is my life now, Trace thought. He was a happily married man, and he had friends and family. If anything, he felt content.

Both of their ranches appeared to be going well, with Trace and Annabelle starting to breed horses as Harlan and Frankie stuck to steers. Harlan said that now the roads were getting easier to and from California, he was even thinking about some sort of coach station or outfitters.

"But I'm going to need a partner. I wouldn't know a thing about where to start." Harlan laughed and nodded at Trace.

"An outfitters?" Trace considered. It made sense, as there were still plenty of wagons taking the trail further west. But one day soon, the railroad would take on that job, wouldn't it? The rails were going to clear a path straight from sea to shining sea, he knew it.

"Post station, or even better, a guest lodge," Trace offered instead. "Where people can stay overnight on their journey. I might be interested in going in with you on something like that."

"You're on," Harlan agreed.

Trace realized that he felt good about the future, and with every passing year, it was only getting better, actually. Colorado City had fewer gun fights now that Cephas was the new sheriff, and he ran a tight group of deputies, with regular training happening every week.

"Then, of course, next year people are talking about the mayorship," Harlan said meaningfully. He nodded in Trace's direction.

"Don't swear at me, Harlan. I have no appetite for the paperwork that comes with that gold chain!" Trace laughed. In truth, he would much rather be a postmaster or an outfitter for the trails than he would be someone who cut ribbons and argued with politicians.

"But *you*, though, brother-in-law," Trace offered right back. "You have a good way with people. Everyone likes you."

Harlan smiled and looked thoughtful. "You know what, maybe I'll do just that."

Just then, the horde of feral children came screaming into the house, with Annabelle and Frankie imploring them to take off their shoes before they trampled dung everywhere.

"Hold it, scamps!" Trace pointed his fingers at Wade, who, even though he was the youngest of their gang, was already turning out to be their natural leader.

"Sorry, Pa," Wade shouted, turning to direct their traffic to the washroom instead.

Trace lifted his head to see Annabelle leaning against the door jamb, looking at him with wonder and amusement in her eyes.

"You look like a man with a new idea, Mr. Flint-Cassidy." Annabelle lifted a careful eyebrow, still smirking.

"Ah, you know me," Trace laughed. He thought about what it would be like, running a trails outfitters station and a ranch at the same time. They had enough ranch hands for the animals right now, and they could stretch to a few more, in all honesty.

It would mean some long hours to get it started, and it would mean meeting all kinds of folk and making them feel safe and welcome.

"Maybe I'm thinking it's about time for our next adventure," Trace grinned.

Annabelle looked at him with a twinkle in her eyes. "Always, husband."

THE END